MEDAL OF HONOR

"I am just going to say a few words
to the Dog. Dog Antis, it gives me great
pleasure to make this presentation for
'outstanding courage, devotion to duty and
life-saving . . .' You are the first foreign
Dog to receive this award, which you
have worthily earned by the steadfastness,
endurance and intelligence for which
your race is well known. You have been
your master's guardian and saviour . . ."

These are excerpts from a speech by
British Field Marshal Lord Wavell as he
awarded Antis the Dickin Medal, the
Animal's Victoria Cross.

This is the story of how that medal was
won. It is a saga of drama and
high adventure you will long remember.
And it is a deeply moving portrait of
a dog you will never forget.

BANTAM PATHFINDER EDITIONS

Bantam Pathfinder Editions provide the best in fiction and nonfiction in a wide variety of subject areas. They include novels by classic and contemporary writers; vivid, accurate histories and biographies; authoritative works in the sciences; collections of short stories, plays and poetry.

Bantam Pathfinder Editions are carefully selected and approved. They are durably bound, printed on specially selected high-quality paper, and presented in a new and handsome format.

ONE MAN
AND HIS DOG

BY ANTHONY RICHARDSON

(Abridged Edition)

BANTAM BOOKS

BANTAM PATHFINDER EDITIONS
NEW YORK / TORONTO / LONDON

RLI: $\dfrac{\text{VLM 7.0}}{\text{IL 7.12}}$

ONE MAN AND HIS DOG

*A Bantam Pathfinder edition / published by arrangement with
E. P. Dutton & Co., Inc.*

PRINTING HISTORY
E. P. Dutton edition published November 1960
Abridged Bantam Pathfinder edition published August 1967

*Bantam Books are published by Bantam Books, Inc., a subsidiary
of Grosset & Dunlap, Inc. Its trade-mark, consisting of the words
"Bantam Books" and the portrayal of a bantam, is registered in the
United States Patent Office and in other countries. Marca Registrada.
Bantam Books, Inc., 271 Madison Avenue, New York, N.Y. 10016.*

PRINTED IN THE UNITED STATES OF AMERICA

CONTENTS

PART ONE *Reveille*

PART TWO *Action Stations*

PART THREE *Last Post*

PART ONE / *Reveille*

chapter i   *"Looking for Someone?"*

1

Once there had been warmth and the comfort of a familiar presence. Now both were gone. A four-week-old Alsatian puppy could scarcely remember ten days ago when his mother had disappeared at one of the first great thunderblasts that had set the farm walls toppling and the farmer and his family scurrying across the snow. Ever since then the thunderblasts had continued, now close at hand, now rumbling in the distance.

Loneliness and a deadly fear had replaced the comfort of his mother's warm tongue that had caressed him while he had suckled with the rest of the litter, which had died with her in that thunderous hour. Thereafter he had lain cold and deserted behind the heap of rubble in the kitchen corner while hunger gnawed at him.

Only a short time ago there had been a very close thunderblast, then a series of explosions and a long, grinding roar. Such sounds struck the utmost terror into his being. They could have turned any dog gun-shy, and already at this early age he was beginning to associate the droning of an airplane's approach with the devastating roar of explosions. That association was to remain with him all the thirteen and a half years of his eventful life.

There was no sound now from the world beyond the rubble heap, and the silence seemed to flow like a tide to the broken walls and flood the room to the sagging ceiling. He struggled shakily to his feet, a rangy puppy.

He snuffled at the heap of plaster before him and attempted to rise on his hind legs, only to fall back on his side. He was too weak from starvation to maintain his balance. He sniffed again at the debris and sneezed. Then, opening his jaws, he gave one long, pitiful, tremulous whine of infinite despair.

It was the morning of February 12, 1940, and the deserted house stood in the no-man's-land between the Maginot and Siegfried lines.

Many feet below, snug in their concrete bastions, the French regiments waited; somewhere opposite German eyes were watching, and no doubt some Britisher across a strip of water was singing about hanging up his washing on the Siegfried Line. But all that was of little consequence to two airmen of the French Air Force, who knew that the last bursts of enemy fire had struck the three-seater Potez 63 in which they were flying.

2

Jan had prophesied trouble if they nosed down through the fog in the valley, but Pierre had wanted to bring photographs back to the base at Nancy. And Serg. Pierre Duval, of the French First Bomber-Reconnaissance Squadron, was, as pilot, captain of the aircraft, and Observer and Air Gunner Jan Bozdech had to abide by the Frenchman's decision.

Now the last burst of red tracer from the German strong post had struck them fair and square. Jan could already see the solid earth and a distant wood, dark against the snow, rushing up to meet them. The Potez 63 was out of control and rapidly losing height.

They struck the ground, bounced, and struck again with the grinding crash of the belly landing, and at terrifying speed skidded across the broken ground. For a second Jan saw the trees of the orchard leaping towards them, and then as the starboard wing struck the ground they were ploughing through the fruit trees. There was a tremendous crashing of branches, and before the darkness overtook him Jan knew that the starboard wing had been torn away.

It was some time before he could see distinctly. The fog seemed to fill his eyes and brain. He felt sick with shock and it was several moments before he could release his harness, clamber out onto the port wing, and slither to the ground.

He lay there panting. Then he began to examine himself inch by inch. There seemed to be nothing broken, though his midriff was bruised. His safety belt had bitten into the flesh on the sudden impact. He remembered on the instant that he had not been alone.

"Pierre," he said. "Where the hell are you?"

There was no answer. It was extraordinarily quiet. Then he saw through a hole in the mist a small, wicked glow of red. He knew at once what he must do.

"Pierre," he was shouting now. A faint sparking glittered through the grey-white haze. He clawed his way back onto the wing.

He could see Pierre now in the pilot's seat. His head was twisted and sagging forward on his chest. Jan thought, The silly bastard, he's broken his bloody neck. A strong smell of petrol set him coughing. A ripple of flame spurted along the fuselage as he snatched at the hatch and flung it open. Fumbling desperately, he released Pierre's harness, and the pilot toppled forward. It was like trying to lift a sack of flour as he dragged his friend clear of his seat. They swayed together on the wing as the tail burst into flames, then both men fell to the snow below.

As he began to drag Pierre clear of the Potez the flames in the far end of the fuselage leapt into the air. His grip tightened. There was no temptation to abandon a comrade, even if his neck was broken. They had flown together for long enough now to warrant their dying together.

Those watching from the distant ridge could probably see the glow of the flames by now, and an enemy patrol would make an end of it, anyway, before help could arrive.

He dragged Pierre for a good twenty yards before the first of the tanks in the burning plane exploded with the detonation of a bomb. The two men lay side by side and the icy touch of the snow on Jan's face, pressed to the ground, was like a benediction. The second tank went up as Pierre began to groan, and a second later the ammunition began to explode.

It was like a miniature bombardment. The bullets hummed past them like hornets. What had once been an aircraft was now a furnace.

"I've hurt my leg," said Pierre suddenly.

"Keep down!" said Jan. "For God's sake, keep down! Never mind your bloody leg!"

"It's my leg," insisted Pierre, "and I've hurt it."

The explosions became desultory. A cloud of black smoke began to drift towards them through the fog.

"I'm sorry about all this," said Pierre.

"Luck of the draw," replied Jan.

The Potez was now a gigantic bonfire, like the festive fire they'd often lit at home in Czechoslovakia around Christmas time. As a boy on his father's estate near Prague, Jan had delighted in this kind of display. But now, as a member of the French forces, he was a proscribed man. If a German patrol captured them it would mean a prisoner-of-war camp for Pierre, but for himself it would mean the firing squad.

"I'm going to leave you here for a minute," said Jan, "and make a recce. We can't stay here."

He crawled forward a dozen yards, and in a sudden lifting of the mist saw the dark outline of a building on the edge of the orchard. Even in that glimpse he could see the shattered roof and the partly demolished side wall. He saw too that no footsteps marked a telltale track in its vicinity. The place seemed deserted. He returned to Pierre.

The latter was sitting up, nursing his leg. There was a dark patch of blood on the snow.

"There's a building over there," said Jan. "Do you think you can make it?"

"Why not?" said Pierre. He grinned cheerfully, but it was more of a grimace than a grin.

"Let's go," said Jan.

They made the passage side by side, on hands and knees, yard by painful yard. There was no sound now from the distant ridge, and the oily smoke from the wrecked aircraft was only a smear in the fog. It took them half an hour to reach the devastated building. The roof gaped to the sky and the front door hung on its hinge.

"Wait here," said Jan. "I'll see if the coast is clear."

He rose to his feet, drew his revolver, and entered the house.

He found himself in what had clearly been the main living room. The table still stood in the center and a sideboard with open drawers and two chairs alongside had suffered no damage. The pictures on the walls hung awry. Thick dust from fallen plaster covered everything. He passed through a door on the right.

An iron range revealed the room as a kitchen. The sink was half full of plaster. An icicle had formed from a dripping tap. He could see the fog through a gaping hole in the ceiling. In the corner a pile of rubble reached knee high. The air was bitterly cold. There was complete silence, except for the creaking front door behind him. He was about to turn on his heel and retrace his footsteps when he heard the slightest of small sounds.

It was, in all that desolate silence, a sinister sound. It made Jan immediately tense his fingers on his revolver. He listened intently. He could hear a faint snuffling, as might arise from a sleeping man. It seemed to come from the corner, where a heap of rubble lay. He waited, tense and alert. The sound stopped.

"You can put up your hands," said Jan loudly. "And come out from wherever you are! No tricks, I've got you covered!"

There was no reply. Silence enveloped him. He could hear the beating of his own heart and his mouth went dry. Then the sound came again, a faint yawning sign that ended in the same snuffle. He stepped forward, his firearm at the ready.

"You can come out and show yourself," he said. "Wake up, you bastard!"

He looked over the pile of rubble, and began to laugh. He had never felt such a fool in his life. Before him crouched a very small dog.

"Hullo," said Jan. "Looking for someone?"

He slipped his revolver into its holster and put out his hand. The puppy struggled to its feet and began to growl.

"That's not the way to greet a friend," said Jan. He liked dogs.

Gently he began to fondle the scruff of the puppy's neck, working his fingers into the loose skin of its coat till they found the base of the ears. The puppy stopped growling and lay bewitched, enchanted. Then at the sound of a footfall, it struggled free, its minute white teeth bared. Jan glanced over his shoulder.

Pierre stood in the doorway, supporting his weight with a hand on the jamb.

"Who are you talking to?" he asked. "What's all the trouble?"

"Here's the trouble," replied Jan, pointing.

3

He had done his best to dress Pierre's leg, slitting up the trouser and washing the wound with his handkerchief dipped in snow water. The bullet had penetrated the flesh of the calf, tearing the muscle and passing through. It was a clean wound and, given a chance, would heal without difficulty. Now Pierre was seated on a chair in the kitchen.

Jan had discovered a hurricane lantern which gave a feeble impression of warmth. The puppy lay in his lap while he sat on the floor studying the outspread map before him.

"Now," said Jan. "I make it seventy-five miles to Nancy, but we've got to get out of this blasted valley first. How's the leg?"

"Aching like hell," said Pierre. "But not so bad as it was."

"There's a wood," said Jan, "about a mile away. It lies practically due west and should be within our territory. So, as soon as it's dark, we'll make for it. It's not safe to move in daylight, even with this fog. German patrols will have been alerted by now."

"And ours as well," said Pierre.

"We can't rely upon that," said Jan. "Do you think you can make it with your leg? ... Lie still, you little brute!"

"Of course I can make it," said Pierre. "Do you think the poor little brute's had anything to eat? He looks half-starved."

"I'm going to look around," said Jan. "Take him a minute, can you?"

He handed over the puppy. When Jan went out, the puppy began to struggle on Pierre's knee, and when he restrained it, to whimper softly.

"Lie still," ordered Pierre. "You haven't had a bullet through you—*yet*."

Jan was back within the minute.

"The fog's still pretty thick," he said. "I hope to God it clears by tonight, otherwise—oh! give the damn thing to me!"

He sat on the floor again, with the puppy on his knee.

"You're a menace," said Jan rubbing its ears. "You'll be the death of us."

"Just what I was thinking," said Pierre. The two men exchanged glances. Jan was the first to look away.

"He's hungry, poor little beast," said Jan.

He groped in his pocket, found his chocolate ration, and held it out to the puppy. It sniffed but made no attempt to eat.

"He's probably not weaned," said Pierre.

"He's got teeth," said Jan.

"How long till dark?" said Pierre.

Jan glanced at his watch.

"Three hours," he replied. "Can you get some rest? I'd help you to the floor, but you might never get up again."

"I'm all right," said Pierre, and winced. "Hell take this bloody leg!"

He lay back in the chair and closed his eyes. Jan drew the puppy closer. Then he softened a piece of chocolate over the lamp. He rubbed it on his forefinger and held it under the dog's nose. The puppy sniffed, and licked the finger clean. The performance was repeated. Seconds later it was eating broken biscuit. Then water, from melted snow, in a battered frying pan left on the stove, and introduced first by the finger tip, taught the puppy to lap. It was a tedious business, but the achievement was a sort of victory.

The time passed very slowly. The little dog slept in Jan's arms. Dogs took to him, just as horses had taken to his mother. He didn't want to think of his mother, nor his father, nor any of the others he'd left behind. One day, he supposed, they would be together again when this wretched war was over. It had all been such a frantic business, confusion upon confusion. He'd escaped from Czechoslovakia to Poland and in Poland he'd enlisted in the Foreign Legion, conditional on his release to the French Air Force in the event of war. His months in the Legion in North Africa had been pretty rough at times. Then there had been the move to France and acceptance in the French Air Force. Now he was fighting the Boche who'd caused all the trouble; that was something. But it was bad luck to be shot down at the outset after all his tribulations.

The puppy stirred and he stroked it as it slept. It was comforting to have something that showed affection and dependence, even if it was only a deserted waif. The puppy licked his hand. The action tugged at his heart-strings.

"God knows what we're going to do with you," he said aloud. But already he knew one thing that they might have to do, and wondered if he could.

At six o'clock he woke Pierre. The fog had lifted. The puppy slept on.

"Ready?" Jan said. "This is it."

"What are we going to do about the dog?" asked Pierre. "We can't take him with us. If we leave him behind he'll starve."

"I've thought of that," said Jan. "I've taught him to eat and drink. No, we can't take him with us. If he starts barking he'll give us away. We'll leave him asleep and board up the door so he can't follow. And we'll leave some rations and water for him. He'll have to take his chance with the rest of us. Do you think you can make it?"

4

The light breeze that had arisen an hour before sunset had lifted the foggy blanket that had covered the valley. Already one or two stars were visible. The moon would rise later. The evening exchange of gunfire had begun. But the accompanying flares were disconcerting. At any moment the white-hot glare of burning magnesium could light up the path of the two airmen making their desperate passage to the silent wood. The only safe method of reaching the fringe of trees was by crawling on hands and knees. There could be no question of Pierre's hobbling along upright with the aid of a supporting arm. It was going to be a slow and painful process.

Only in the orchard adjoining the derelict farm did they dare stand upright, and then it was to drop hastily into the ditch on the far side as another flare spluttered almost overhead.

Before leaving the farm Jan had slung the front door slantwise across the entrance. Behind it they had left the puppy still sleeping, with provisions by its side.

The flare above the orchard slowly began to sink. Both men lay flat on their faces on the far side of the ditch. The flashes of German guns increased, and the rumble of their detonations shook the air. They instinctively knew the moment had arrived to leave the ditch.

And then, distinctly to be heard above the muttering of the guns, came the sound which Jan had all along subconsciously dreaded—the yapping of a deserted dog!

It was perfectly clear what must be done. There were no two ways about it. Jan felt for his knife. To use his revolver and risk the sound of a shot would be madness. By now the roving night patrols would be out listening in the snow.

"Wait there," he whispered to Pierre. "I'll be back in a minute."

He spoke collectedly, as a man excusing himself on a habitual errand, but to himself his voice sounded unfamiliar.

"Sorry," said Pierre, with his typical, quick sympathy, "but we have no other choice."

Jan crawled back across the ditch and reached the first of the fruit trees. Then he rose and blundered forward. He passed through the neat rows of lime-washed trunks. A distant flare went up. Then he heard the sound of a small body hurling itself against the low barricade. Two forelegs momentarily hung over the edge while the hindlegs scrabbled to find a hold. Then the forelegs slipped back. As he waited, irresolute, the maneuver was repeated, only this time he caught a glimpse of the small head and the pointed nose and heard the anguished panting. He took another silent step forward and peered over the top of the broken door. For the second time that day, dog and man stared at one another.

Jan turned from the barrier to search for a stick or a stone. He felt he must have a small log or a large stone, because it was unthinkable to kill a dog with a knife. It was murder. But a crack across the skull could first send the poor brute unconscious. He could find neither stone nor log—the snow covered everything.

He became agitated, assailed by panic. He must get on with the job before the puppy yelped again. Pierre was waiting for him, his leg hurting like hell. The Germans had done that. The Germans had tried to kill as he had tried to kill. Only that was man's recognized inhumanity to man. That was accepted. But to kill a dog with a knife! How did anyone go about it?

He heard a whine from the other side of the door. The last shreds of his resolution snapped.

"Oh, hell!" cursed Jan.

He flung aside the barrier, unfastened his flying jacket, put the unresisting puppy inside, against his breast, and made his way back to Pierre.

5

The moon was up. Its light confused and hindered their progress. It would disappear behind the fleecy clouds rising high in the icy air, and people the valley with shadows. Each shadow could have been the movement of a patrol.

Pierre had little comment to make about the puppy. He had only said:

"I thought when you set off that I was glad it was you and not me."

Now for the moment the rumbling guns seemed to have drifted to the east. From time to time at a burst of machine-gun fire, both men would crouch lower in whatever cover was available. When a flare lit the sky or the machine-gunning drew closer they lay flat on their faces. When the sky darkened and the chatter of weapons died away they crawled forward again.

During a pause in the ebb and flow of the guns, Jan glanced at his watch. They had been half an hour on their journey. Knees and hands were becoming painfully sore. Where the layer of snow was thin, an unexpected pebble could produce agony. Pierre, he felt certain, must be enduring the torments of the damned.

The gunfire momentarily sank to a mutter. The moon was behind a cloud. He nudged Pierre, and they both rose a little. They had crawled scarcely four paces when a flare crackled almost immediately over their heads. They both sprawled flat in the snow. The flare was so low that Jan felt certain it had actually been aimed in their direction.

He hugged the ground, his fingers and toes digging into the inhospitable earth. He had flung himself down with considerable force, but he could still feel the movement of the puppy against his chest.

Under the crook of his elbow Jan could see Pierre's left hand, in his white glove. He reached out and gave the hand a reassuring grasp.

"For God's sake, lie still," whispered Pierre.

As the flare sank, a burst of rifle fire split the air. He expected to feel the draught of a stream of bullets across the nape of his neck. When none came he raised his head a couple of inches.

Bullets were ricocheting in showers off the metal skeleton of the Potez. He knew then that they were not alone in the valley, that somebody else too was astir. Then the flare still burning, fell to the ground not twenty yards away, and the rifle fire ceased. For what seemed an eternity, beyond the muffled undertone of the now faraway guns, there was silence. In a little time they continued on their way.

By midnight they were within a hundred yards of their goal. The struggle up the slope taxed Pierre nearly to his limit. He had fallen, and it was proving almost impossible for him to get up again.

"Go on ahead," he urged. "Leave me. You'll run into some of our people and then you can come back for me."

His head dropped into the snow.

"Nobody's leaving anybody," said Jan.

The puppy began to struggle at the opening of his jacket.

"And that goes for you, too," said Jan, and pressed the dog's head back in place. A small, warm tongue licked his fingers. He moved closer to Pierre and put his arms round him, his hand in the other's armpit.

"When you feel me shove, try to move. We're nearly there."

They made their way up the last ninety yards, side by side, clinging to the ground. They progressed, literally, by inches. It took them three-quarters of an hour to reach the foot of the first tree. Jan hauled his companion behind a great fir that leaned out towards them like the bowsprit of a ship. The cannonade was increasing again, but Pierre rolled over on his back and was fast asleep in a second.

Jan chose a tall tree and sank down with his back to it. Every muscle in his body was on fire. He fumbled for the opening of his jacket, took the puppy out, and held it on his lap. It was, surprisingly, none the worse for its journey.

He put his arms round the little animal and held it close. It made no attempt to struggle, but searched with its hind paws for a purchase to draw still closer. From time to time it looked up at him and once when he moved, it licked his chin.

Jan lay back against the tree trunk in a semicoma. The sound of the guns died away. The freezing valley and the dark wood were utterly silent. The two exhausted men lay as the dead. Only the puppy revealed any sign of life. It shifted its position, shivering, till Jan replaced it in his jacket for warmth. Then, satisfied that their world was undisturbed, it lay against Jan's breast and fell asleep.

By one o'clock in the morning the cold woke Pierre. He called softly to Jan, "Wake up. Are you all right?"

Jan rose, for the moment doubled up with cramp. Then he went over to his companion.

"How's the leg?"

"Better now I've had a rest. The cold seems to have numbed the pain a bit. I shall be all right now."

"We ought to get going. We don't want to be caught by the daylight. But we must be within our own patrol area by now."

"Have you still got the dog?" asked Pierre.

"He's as good as gold," answered Jan. "Never a squeak out of him."

"Time yet," said Pierre.

The puppy, his head just out of Jan's jacket, gave a low whine.

"What's the matter?" said Jan. "You're a damn silly dog, aren't you?"

The puppy growled again, his ears pricked.

"Quiet now," said Jan.

"Listen," hissed Pierre urgently. "The dog can hear something we can't."

They listened to the silence. Then, like a pistol shot, a twig snapped. Jan stifled the bark in the dog's throat with a hand across its muzzle. The two men looked around them. The trees stood thick and dark. Snow suddenly slithered from a branch to the ground with a thud. Pierre tried to gain his feet.

As Jan moved forward to help him three men stepped out from the trees. Two bayonets glistened at Jan's throat. A third swept in a half-arc to menace Pierre. In every place where a tree had stood now an armed man seemed to stand.

Now that the dreaded moment had arrived all sense of disaster left Jan. There was nothing to be done. It had been the worst of unlucky days. Now he could only feel relief.

Someone moved out of the gloom. It was an officer in French uniform.

"Who are you?"

It was important to speak quickly, Jan told himself, but he was tongue-tied with joy. Then he heard Pierre.

"Sergeant Duval. French First Bomber-Reconnaissance Squadron."

Jan found his voice. It didn't sound like his own.

"Sergeant Bozdech. Observer and Air Gunner. We were shot down this morning, sir. My pilot is wounded."

"Make a litter for this airman."

Two soldiers made an improvised stretcher of rifles and a greatcoat, and helped Pierre on.

The party moved off. The entire business was completed in silence. Jan walked at Pierre's side like a man in a dream. In a little time the trees were gone and they came to a blockhouse heavily camouflaged with concrete emplacements on either side.

The officer ranged up alongside.

"We were out looking for you. You were seen to go in this morning. It is well met."

"It is excellently well met, sir," said Jan, with enthusiasm.

"Is your pilot badly wounded?"

"Through the leg, sir. A bullet. He will recover."

"Anyone who can get up that slope with a bullet through his leg will recover. You are both to be congratulated. You will stay here tonight. In the morning Sergeant Duval will be taken to hospital. We can give him only first aid here. But you will both have a meal and a bed and be comfortable."

"Thank you, sir."

"And you will be driven to your base tomorrow. At——— —?"

"At St. Dizier, attached Nancy, sir."

They were entering the door of the blockhouse.

"What's that you've got there?"

"A dog, sir. A puppy."

"Bring him in with you. Have you had him long?"

"Long enough to make friends with him, sir," said Jan with a grin.

6

Pierre was gone by the time Jan awoke the next morning. There had been no need to disturb him, they said. Pierre had left his love and said he would be back with the Squadron in no time. A Renault was waiting to take Jan back to Haguenau, they said, and from there he'd be flown the remaining hundred and fifteen miles to St. Dizier in a Potez 25. The two-seater training airplane would be just the thing to introduce the puppy to the air. It was a pity Jan's visit must be so curtailed, but after all, there was a war on their hands, even if it didn't seem much like it at the moment. It was boring to sit and wait for the Boche to make up his mind what he was going to do. Maybe he had already decided to go back home. It was one thing advancing up to his own lines with all the glitter and glamor of war and to bomb open cities and kill defenseless civilians, but another to come up against the steel and concrete might of the Maginot Line. Most certainly that was a very different thing, and time would show that. And so, *au revoir,* and don't forget the little dog. *Au revoir,* and their greetings to their comrades-in-arms of the French Air Force. And look after the little puppy, but they felt sure, after hearing the romantic story, that he was in good hands.

1

Seven exiles of Czechoslovakia were all members of the First Bomber-Reconnaissance Squadron of the French Air Force, stationed at St. Dizier, fifty-three miles from Nancy. All had been members of the Czech Air Force before Hitler invaded their country. All had served as Legionnaires in the North African desert at Sidi-bel-Abbes. All were fired with the same spirit, to strike back at all costs against the Germans.

There was Joska, twenty-four and a crack shot; handsome Karel was twenty-three; Ludva, the adventurous, was nicknamed "Flame" because of his red hair; serious Josef, twenty-six, was also skilled with a pistol; Gustav, only eighteen, had a way with girls; Vlasta, the father of the party at thirty-two, was a man of good sense and initiative; and lastly there was Jan, twenty-six, who as a former member of the Czech Air Force had represented his service at athletics. And now there was the dog.

They had all had a party to celebrate Jan's return. They lived in a blockhouse near the airfield and at night, so intense was the cold, they slept in their greatcoats. But nothing could stop them from having a party when they had a mind to, if it was only on beer. They drank considerably, in honor of the occasion and of the newcomer who sat at Jan's feet and to whom they had taken a very great fancy.

"But what are you going to call him?" said Karel. "A dog's got to have a name."

They all made suggestions but none of them suited.

When they had come to a deadlock Joska had a sudden brain wave.

"We ought to have a name," he suggested, "which is suitably unique, short, and which is typically personal to us, being our dog."

"My dog," said Jan.

"Why not name him after our beloved A.N.T. bombers at home and call him Ant?"

"Not Ant," said Karel. "That is not quite distinguished enough. Let's make it Antis."

So the puppy was christened with beer, instead of champagne, by a name that was to stick.

The weeks passed and the puppy flourished and grew, and being intelligent and lovingly instructed, by the end of February had to learn to shake hands with each of the friends. Because of the weather and lack of opportunity, hours in the air were disappointingly rare. Every night the dog slept in the blockhouse at Jan's feet.

Rumors were daily increasing that the Germans were preparing for an offensive in the spring. But to the French, smug and complacent within their impregnable Maginot Line, such a threat was but a vapor.

So Jan was readily granted fourteen days' leave in Paris, beginning March 10 to meet a pen friend with whom, through the good offices of the Czech Consulate, he had long corresponded. The lady's name was Yvette.

2

Antis, at two months, was accustomed to the company of men, but his rapidly growing mind was beginning to center on Jan, who alone fed and tended him.

There had been no earlier need to tie the dog up or put him on a lead, but with the visit to a town imminent, Jan bought a collar and hung on it his Foreign Legion identity disk which was registered with the French police.

Then they set off for Paris. They met Yvette at the appointed place and took rooms for a fortnight in the Rue de L'Espérance.

For the first three days it promised to be a good leave. On the morning of the fourth day Jan took the girl out to lunch. They left the dog dozing on the rug in the sitting room. At the last minute, as they were about to climb into a taxi, Yvette found that her bag was missing. Jan hastily ran back, found the bag, slammed the door after him, and returned to the lady. The lock failed to connect and the door was left ajar.

At three o'clock the couple returned. It had been till then a highly successful occasion. Jan saw Yvette to her room to rest for the evening's outing, and made his way to his own. Outside it had begun to drizzle. Jan opened his door and called the password, "Looking for someone?" There was none of the usual commotion in response. The sitting room seemed unbelievably empty.

He went into his bedroom, calling the dog by name. Under the bed, in the wardrobe, behind the dressing table, there was no sign of Antis.

He dreaded to think what might have happened. He tried to recapitulate his movements. Each time he failed to remember the crucial point in the sequence. Had or had he not locked the door? Frustration, panic, and fury filled him. This was the sort of thing that would happen. He was getting on famously with Yvette. He wanted no distractions such as this. The dog was a damn nuisance. He wished that he hadn't brought him with him. He voiced his opinion out loud. "Damn the dog!"

The sound of his own voice startled him. After all, the dog had only followed his natural instincts of loyalty and devotion. The dog had missed him and tried to follow him. His was the fault. Therefore he must search and find the dog. If he was unable to keep tonight's date with Yvette, that would be just too bad. He was beginning to discover where his heart really lay.

He went to the janitor's room. The man had chosen this hour for a nap and disliked being disturbed.

"No, I've not seen any dog. I don't want to see any dogs, anyway. We don't like them here."

He shut the door in Jan's face.

Jan searched the garden at the back of the house, but there was no sudden rush across the lawn or out of the shrubbery, so he made his way into the street. Scores of pedestrians, on inquiry, had certainly never seen a dog of that description. At five o'clock Jan was interviewing the sergeant in charge at the police station. Nobody had reported finding such a dog, nor had one been brought in. Soon Yvette would be arising from her siesta.

Remembering his military training, but not Yvette, Jan began a tour of the streets, walking a good mile in a set direction, and then, as the topography permitted, making a concentrated search in diminishing circles till he reached his own front door. His efforts brought no success.

His rooms were still deserted except for Yvette, dressed for the evening, who asked brightly if he liked walking in the rain and wasn't it time to get started. Jan replied that he'd lost his dog. It was a phrase which he was beginning to find irksome. Yvette said she was very sorry, but was a dog more important than she was? Jan, worried to distraction and taken off his guard, said that for the moment that could very well be the case and please would she try to understand? She went to the door and let herself out. Jan sat on the sofa and started swearing again. Then in a despairing last resort he went back to the police station. Another sergeant was on duty, an amiable man and intelligent. Jan asked if there weren't some way of advertising to let the world know he'd lost his dog.

The sergeant said, "Try a police broadcast. The fee won't be more than a hundred francs." He picked up the telephone there and then and arranged for a broadcast that evening for no fee at all.

Jan spent the night alone. There was neither Antis nor Yvette to comfort him. It was the dog's company he would have preferred.

He rose for breakfast with a heart as heavy as lead. There were eleven more days to go before his leave ended but he would be glad of the sight of the St. Dizier airdrome at this very moment. Or would he? There would be anxious inquiries about the dog from Ludva and Joska and Karel and all the rest. There was nothing he would be able to say. Antis was lost by his negligence. They would all be pretty sore about it and rightly so. And then, from somewhere down below, he thought he heard a bark.

He ran to the door and flung it open. There were voices on the floor beneath, and footsteps coming up the stairs. The postman appeared at the head of the first flight. Straining at the cord tied to his collar, panting, his jaws gaping, was Antis. The postman dropped his end of the cord, and the dog hurtled down the corridor and sprang into Jan's arms as he knelt to receive him. Dog and man merged together.

"Thank God," said Jan, holding the dog's muzzle from his face to avoid the tongue that was licking its wild welcome.

"He seems to know his master," observed the postman, looking on indulgently. "I found him lying exhausted in the Avenue Kléber. He looked as if he'd been out all night. He was in a poor way. I picked him up and took him to the police and they sent me on here."

"Come in," cried Jan. "Come in and have a drink."

"At this early hour it would not usually be my custom, but if monsieur insists, on an occasion such as this, maybe a little cognac—"

He followed Jan and his dog into the sitting room.

Half an hour later Yvette appeared. She too had experienced a sleepless night. She didn't want there to be any misunderstanding.

Jan said there wasn't and there never had been and sat her down on the sofa beside him, and the dog sat and looked from one to another because there was never any knowing what these humans might do next. But the postman seemed to know because he swallowed his third glass of brandy with speed and then, all smiles and *bonhomie,* excused himself and went out, shutting the door very securely behind him.

For the next eleven days, Jan saw Yvette evenings. In the daytime he trained Antis to keep close heel and then to follow, head abreast of his own left knee, without the lead. By the end of his leave Antis could find his master in a crowd when the latter had deliberately dodged him, and had learned to come to the signal whistle without hesitation.

3

In April 1940 Hitler invaded Norway and Denmark. On May 10 the German forces poured into Holland, Belgium, and Luxembourg.

The French armies moved up into Belgium, but the Panzer Divisions swept on. On May 14 the Maginot Line was breached at Sedan and the crossing of the Meuse began. The seven Czech friends had been posted to Mézières which was immediately bombed and made unserviceable. The airmen did not even unpack before leaving for La Malmaison, where they hoped for respite. But the situation had so deteriorated that none of the Squadron knew on take-off where they would land on return. Determined not to risk separation, Jan decided that Antis must fly with him on all sorties to which they were assigned. The dog behaved perfectly, lying at Jan's feet dozing for most of the time. Despite the inevitable casualties in the squadron, the seven Czechs seemed to bear charmed lives, until May 21. Karel's Bloch 200 Bomber was shot down when attacking German columns as they crossed the Somme.

That night at La Malmaison, Antis wandered disconsolate from one to another of the six surviving friends, looking in vain for the airman who had failed to return. The following morning, on his way to Squadron headquarters, Jan, to his amazed delight, encountered Pierre. His former pilot, his wound now healed, had been pursuing his old Squadron, now reduced to a flight, from one airdrome to the next. The day after, to add still more to Jan's delight, on returning from a mission, he found Karel awaiting him. The pilot of the Bloch 200 had luckily managed to land in a field near Amiens.

The flying crews were rapidly becoming exhausted. On June 11, the Squadron was told that Italy had declared war on France. By June 12, the Germans were reported to have reached Beauvais and Senlis, twenty miles from Paris. By the middle of the month the entire French Armies were on the run as the Germans swept south. Roads became blocked; no prisoners of war were taken, but all those captured were disarmed and allowed to wander at will, each man for himself in a desperate and generally hopeless endeavor to find his way home. The result was completely demoralizing.

The confusion spread. The roads now became jammed with refugees. Parisians in luxurious cars struggled with outmoded models from Brussels. At the first indication of enemy action from the air the occupants of all cars, the remains of their belongings piled high on the roof, scuttled panic-stricken for the roadside ditches.

On June 14 Paris was occupied by the enemy. All that remained of Jan's flight was rapidly transferred from Chartres to Châteaudun. The seven Czechs were still together and the dog was still of their company.

At Châteaudun they were told that the enemy Panzers were only eight miles away. They set off again towards Le Breuil. It was to prove their last destination. As the surviving air crews and ground crews worked on their aircraft ten German ME. 109's swept across the airdrome and attacked. All the remaining French aircraft were destroyed on the ground.

On the following evening on the outskirts of Le Breuil, the Adjutant called together all survivors. Sixty exhausted men of all ranks mustered under the trees in the garden of a farm. Overhead the enemy fighters circled and searched.

The roll call was taken. Each man was paid and issued with six days' ration of bread, sardines, and chocolate.

Then, with a shaking hand, the Adjutant read out the last message to be received from the French Army Headquarters. Eighty-four-year-old Marshal Pétain, Premier of France, had asked the Germans for an armistice.

"Gentlemen," said the Adjutant, "it is now every man for himself. The enemy is already in Orleans and advancing on Blois, which is only eight miles distant. The nearest station for any train that may still be running to the south is twenty-five miles away at Tours. God be with you. We shall meet again and fight again."

It was the end.

4

Since a concerted escape was impossible, the sixty men split up into groups, friends and associates choosing to keep together. Jan's party consisted of his six fellow Czechs and Antis, and the two Frenchmen, Pierre Duval and his friend Jacques Chevalier.

They withdrew to a corner of the garden. It was approaching five o'clock on a warm, sultry evening. High overhead they could see yet another enemy formation.

"Before we make a move," said Vlasta, "we've got to have a plan. I don't know about you people, but my mind's made up."

"We're listening," said Karel. "You've generally been right in the past."

From where they stood they could see the road through the village. It was congested with traffic of every kind, creeping at a snail's pace: limousines, carts, lorries, pedestrians, and even a man riding a horse. A shout from the rear sent everyone running into the shelter of doorways. A German fighter roared across the column at two hundred feet without opening fire. An old man stood, face upraised, shaking his fist. The bonnet of the car behind bumped him viciously in the back. He stumbled and staggered on. A bald-headed, bearded man, with two expensive ladies in his Renault, leaned out to scream at those ahead. A piano broke its ropes and slid off the back of a truck, shattering the wooden porch of a cottage. Surprisingly, a laughing child ran into the garden, plucked a flower, and waved to Jan.

"Well, I'm not giving up," said Vlasta. "To hell with Marshal Pétain and the rest of his bog rats."

"I couldn't agree more," said Josef. "We came here to fight the bloody Germans, not run away."

Everyone joined in a chorus of assent.

"I suggest," said Vlasta, "we stick together and try and get to England. We'll fight on from there."

"And how do we get there?" said Joska.

"We do it in stages. We've got to get a train for Sète. The Czech Army Depot is nineteen miles from Sète, and once we're there we shall know what our own people are doing. They may even be running boats to England."

"And if there aren't any boats?" said Ludva.

"Then we'll fly. Somewhere amid all this panic and chaos somebody will have forgotten an airplane—we can borrow it."

"That's what I like to hear," said Jan.

"If the Germans don't get there first," put in Josef.

"That's a chance we've got to accept," said Ludva.

"All right," said Vlasta. "That's settled then. We'll get back to our billet and collect our kit."

"Let's go," said Karel. Then he held up a hand, listening.

A sound was becoming audible, a clattering rumble and highpitched whine of changing gears.

"Tanks," said Karel shortly. "On our way, then."

They made their way to the barn where they had slept for the last three nights. The farmer's wife with her two children tugging at her skirt watched them, dabbing her eyes with the corner of her apron.

In a quarter of an hour all nine had collected their two suitcases apiece, and stood once more in the farmyard. The farmer came out of his cart shed and joined his wife

and children, who still waited to make their final farewells. He shook his head mournfully.

"You'll never manage to carry all that lot," he said to
Jan.

"We'll cope," said Jan.

"Not at that pace," said the farmer, and jerked his head
in the direction of the stream of traffic passing his gate.
"Come with me."

He turned back into his shed and lifted the shafts of
any old pony trap and began to wheel it out.

"You're welcome to this," he said. "It's better than
nothing."

He helped them pile their suitcases in the well of the
trap. Their flying kit was placed across the seats. When
the load was complete Jan motioned to Antis and the dog
obediently took his place on the top of the pile. In that
fashion they passed out of the farmyard to join the refugee
column.

The last they saw of their good friend was leaning over
his gate waving to them.

"Bon voyage," he called. *"Bon voyage."*

But his wife was still weeping.

5

The pace of the column was agonizingly slow. The road
narrowed and the congestion doubled with nightfall. The
interlocked mass of vehicles and humanity seeped between
the confines of the bordering ditches like mud through an
inadequate culvert. Night had fallen an hour ago.

Many of the refugees, indifferent to danger, now sought
the grass, hauling their mattresses down from the roofs of
their cars. They lay, oblivious in their misery to the menac-
ing sound of gunfire in the rear. Families huddled together for warmth, and above the grinding of wheels the cries
of the children could be heard.

Towards midnight Karel said, "This is no good. We're not getting anywhere. The guns are nearer. The Boche is overtaking us."

Each of the men knew what was in his mind. As Czechs, they were proscribed men. They could be shot out of hand. Soon the advancing Panzers would close the escape route. Time was pressing hard.

"There's only one thing to do. We've got to get out of this mob. It may be rough going, but our only chance is to take to the fields," continued Karel. "We can keep a parallel course with the road. It's the only way we can save time."

They chose the next gate. Vlasta, who carried a pocket compass, set the course. There was no knowing what obstacles they might meet, but the menace of the armored columns in pursuit drove them on. Even now some advance units of the enemy might be ahead of them. At any moment they could expect to hear the harsh shout of a challenge in German.

The going was appalling. Over the rough ground the cart lurched from side to side. The dog, clawing desperately to retain his foothold, began to whine in his distress. When Josef, now at the shafts, slipped and fell, the trap tilted back and the dog fell heavily to the ground. Jan picked him up and put him back on top of the baggage. He immediately began to whine again.

"Keep that damn dog quiet," whispered Vlasta. His voice was harsh with tension.

Somewhere, ahead of them, was movement. At any moment the blinding headlights of an enemy patrol could reveal them. Then they were among a herd of cattle. The trap went over on its side and the dog fell off again. They reloaded the cart, and Jan placed Antis on the corner of a seat. They passed through the herd. Both Karel and Jacques tripped over the low, wooden water trough in the dark. Nobody spoke. They could still hear the refugee column, but the sound of the advancing Panzers was still louder.

Antis began to fall from the trap at the least lurch. His

whine was becoming continuous. Each time he fell, Jan had to pick him up again. The precious moments lost began to mount up. On each occasion Vlasta would examine the face of his luminous wristwatch.

As Antis fell once again and broke into a low howl the older man's nerve momentarily snapped.

"That bloody dog will be the death of us," he said loudly. "We must get rid of him. Let me have him."

He lunged forward, but Jan was too quick for him. He snatched the dog from Vlasta's grasping fingers and tucked Antis under his own arm. They walked on in silence.

The dog was heavy. This was no longer a puppy to be carried within a flying jacket, and in a very short time Jan was finding it necessary to shift his burden from one arm to another at intervals of fifty yards. He bore no grudge against Vlasta, his friend. That Vlasta should be the first to break under the tension of this terrible night was far more disconcerting than his involuntary outburst. The endless days of retreat, frustration, and defeat were taking their toll. Then he felt a touch on his free arm and Vlasta was whispering in his ear.

"Forgive what I said. Let me carry the dog for a bit. You're all in."

Jan handed Antis over without a word.

At midnight they rested. For the moment they could go no farther. Each swallowed a mouthful of wine, then dropped to the ground exhausted. Jan told himself that the struggle up the valley slope with Pierre had been nothing compared to this desperate passage through the dark. There the tumult of battle had been stationary behind him; now, with every minute that passed, its sound drew closer. The menace of pursuit was becoming intolerable. So, he supposed, it had always been in the retreats of wars, when men had dropped by the wayside, too deadened by fatigue to care further if they lived or died.

The sounds of machine guns and armored vehicles had now become part of the night with the friendly sounds of owl and cricket and lowing kine. Now another sound, very faint, was intruding upon those others. It was the distant but unmistakable hiss of a locomotive getting up steam.

Jan dragged himself to his feet. The others were also stirring at this unexpected message of hope, so that Jan voiced the opinion of them all.

"I hear an engine in a siding," he said.

"And so do I," said Karel. "It's over to our left."

"Come on," said Vlasta. "That's the way we take."

They followed the sound for half a mile with renewed impetus. Then, as they rounded the corner of a lane, they came upon the station. The sound of the engine was appreciably nearer.

"It's too good to be true," breathed Vlasta.

But Gustav was already running down the platform. Then, with the cart in their midst and Antis at his master's side, they began their assault on the dark and silent building. They rattled the doors, banged on the shutters, and shouted.

There was no response. They crowded round and peered into the unlit booking-office window.

"Stand back," said Pierre and aimed a wicked blow with his elbow. The glass fragments fell with a crash into the interior of the office. A window was flung open on the floor above. A voice said:

"What do you think you're doing?"

From the platform they could see a tousled head above a window sill. The owner of the head repeated his question with feeling.

"And there are no more trains, anyway. So you are wasting your time," he added, preparing to shut out the night.

"We are nine airmen of the French Air Force—we need help," cried Pierre.

"I tell you—there are no more trains."

"Then what's that we've been hearing for the last half hour?" demanded Ludva. "There's a train getting up steam somewhere near here. You've got to help us. The Boche is right on our tail."

"There may be a train in the siding two miles down the line. Follow the track past the signals. If your luck's in you may get aboard."

The window began to close.

"Thank you!" said Pierre. "We can't thank you enough."

"Oh! Go to hell!" said the voice from above.

The window shut with a crash.

The journey down the track seemed unending. The cart jolted and bumped till they thought the springs would fall apart. Halfway across a small bridge the first challenge of the night rang out.

"Halt! Who goes there?"

"Friend," called Pierre.

"Advance, friend, and be recognized."

Pierre went forward alone.

"There's a party with you," said the sentry. "Who are they?"

"Eight other members of the French Air Force," said Pierre.

"What do you want?" said the sentry.

"A train," replied Pierre.

"So does the rest of the world tonight," said the sentry. "What's the password?"

"We don't know," said Pierre.

Faintly and far-off, but unmistakably, came the rumble of tanks.

"I can't let you through without the password," said the sentry. "Orders is orders."

"And Panzers are Panzers," said Pierre.

"There's no answer to that," conceded the sentry, and gave the password.

Four times again they needed the password before at last the train stood in full view. It consisted of some thirty carriages and trucks, and boasted three engines at the head. It seemed significant to Jan of the general disorganization that such a load should be drawn with so much power forward and with none in the rear in support.

It was now bright starlight and a crescent moon had

appeared. On either side of the track scores of men, women, and children shouted, struggled, and fought for seats in a train already packed with refugees from Belgium and the north of France. No quarter was given. The old, the very young, and the crippled were thrust aside by the strong and ruthless. The scene was to remain in Jan's memory for very many days.

But they found, at last, an empty corner in a cattle truck, containing a Belgian woman and her two daughters.

By three o'clock in the morning, they were ensconced with their baggage in the wagon. The cart lay abandoned with scores of other vehicles at the side of the line.

At dawn the thirty carriages began to move. The airmen sat with their backs against the filthy sides of the truck. The dog, ravenously devouring his share of sardines, lay with his head in the lap of the elder of the two Belgian girls.

As the train gathered speed Ludva the irrepressible, raised his voice and shouted:

"All aboard for the Riviera Express. *En voiture! En voiture!* First stop Sète!"

And everybody, for the first time for many hours, laughed out loud.

chapter iii   *Escape to Gibraltar*

1

Over a week had passed since they boarded the train and since they had eaten a proper meal. Now at Nîmes during an eighteen-hour delay, they decided to find some real food. To their astonishment, they discovered the restaurant Prague Suburb.

At first the proprietor looked askance at the nine disheveled ruffians till Karel revealed their nationality. Then the old man provided a typical Czechoslovakian feast: smoked pork, cabbage, and dumplings, followed by a small cake and black coffee. And an immense steak and a bowl of milk for Antis.

They entertained the old man and his wife with the story of their train journey south. It had taken three days to cover the sixty miles to Moulins. First the train had broken in two because there had been no engine in the rear, and then a carriage axle had broken. Air attacks and air-raid warnings and bombed tracks had all occasioned frequent delays.

Once a bread train had pulled in behind them, a great piece of luck because many refugees were almost starving. Antis had begun to hide at the sound of a tin being opened, he was so tired of sardines and chocolate. Finally Jan found a baby's bottle; since milk was distributed at the stations for children, it had only been necessary to display the bottle out of the window. The deception had worked until Antis had bitten off the nipple and swallowed it. Then it became much harder to renew his supply of milk.

On June 24 they had seen the crowd at Bessay dancing

and singing because they had been told that Russia had declared war on Germany. All agreed that it was a terrible disappointment when the news proved false, because it would have meant so much to stricken France. For the next day at Vichy, they heard the loud-speakers blaring Pétain's "Lay Down Your Arms" broadcast, urging people to return to their homes. Only a few had taken his advice.

But after that the lights had come on in the train and there were no more air-raid warnings or damaged tracks to repair. Compared to their former progress, the train had flown along. At Bironde, the Belgian woman had left with her two daughters. Antis had missed his good friend, the elder girl. And so it had gone until this wonderful moment when they'd eaten this magnificent meal which they would never, never forget.

"And now," said Vlasta to the proprietor, "what do we owe you?"

They all looked at one another in some trepidation, because after the minor but frequent expenses of their journey the money remaining between them in the "kitty" would surely be insufficient to meet the bill for all the munificent fare that had been set before them.

"What do you intend to do now?" inquired the proprietor, ignoring Vlasta's question.

"We're all agreed that we're going to fight on from England," replied Ludva.

"Bravo!" said the proprietor, himself an old soldier.

"What's the news of the Czech Army?" said Karel. "We're making for Sète."

"Sète's the place," said the proprietor. "Our people are being shipped out of there every day."

"That's tremendous news," said Ludva. "All aboard for Sète!"

"Your bill, if you please," said Vlasta.

"Am I to be deprived of the privilege of helping my fellow countrymen, who will one day help to drive the Germans from my adopted land?" said the proprietor. "Don't be absurd, there is nothing to pay!"

They said good-by, wringing the old man's hand till his arms ached and the last they saw of him was outside his restaurant door, waving farewell with one hand, while his other was round his wife's shoulders.

"All aboard for Sète!" cried Ludva, beside himself.

They climbed aboard the train for the short run to Montpellier, *en route* for their final destination.

2

They bade farewell to Pierre and Jacques at Montpellier. It was not so painful a parting as they had anticipated. The effect of the hospitality of the Prague Suburb was still with them, and journey's end seemed near. Each would see this ugly business through. They were full of fight.

They stood on the platform awaiting the train for Sète. It would not be very long now before they were reunited with many of their fellow exiles in the transit unit, prepared for them probably at Agde, where the former Czech depot had been. Time was doubtless on their side. The Germans' influence would now be rapidly spreading to the south, but nevertheless, it would still take time to close the net completely. They discussed their chances with growing optimism as they waited for their train. Hope ran high.

It was Josef, standing a little apart from the others, whom the infantryman in battle dress first approached. He had been standing with his wife and two children by their baggage. He greeted Josef in Czechoslovakian and Josef at once called to Jan:

"Here is another of us."

They formed a circle round the soldier. Now there would be firsthand news. They began to question him eagerly. Did he know the depot at Agde? What was the news from Sète?

But he was getting out of uniform as soon as he could,

returning to his home in Paris with his family, and forgetting the war. His news was crushing.

"As far as we're concerned, the war is over," he said. "If I were you, I should get out of that uniform very quickly. We are not looked on with favor by the Germans."

"Tell me," said Vlasta, "are there boats running from Sète for England—"

"The last boat left Sète harbor four days ago," said the soldier. "The harbor is closed to outgoing ships. There is my train. I must go. Take my advice. Get out of that uniform. You are marked men. Good-by and good luck!"

He turned on his heel and left them.

There was a moment of stunned silence among the seven. Ludva had gone very white. He looked like a small boy who had just been whipped. Jan put his hand down to find his dog.

"If that's true," said Gustav, in a husky whisper, "we're done. We're finished. We're dead men!"

"I don't believe it," said Karel in a very loud voice. "I'm not going to believe it. We'll steal a boat. Or an airplane. It's a bloody lie!"

"The train for Sète's coming in," said Vlasta gently.

"Then get aboard," said Karel violently. "Get aboard, the whole damn lot of you! What's the matter with you? Get a move on."

He turned to Vlasta.

"It's a lie, isn't it?" he said brokenly. "Tell me it's a bloody lie."

His voice cracked.

"We'll go and see," said Vlasta quietly. "Come along, Karel, all of you—we'll go and see."

3

They reached Sète at three o'clock in the afternoon. The train was on time, which was very creditable. At the station they were told that the last convoy, carrying Czech refugees to England, had left four days ago, on June 25.

They made their way down to the harbor. It was very quiet. One or two fishing boats rode at their moorings and a cloud of sea gulls screeched and dipped. Even the ancient houses on the water front had a blind look, like old crones dozing with half-closed eyes.

"This place gives me the creeps," said Gustav. "Let's go to that café and talk."

They trooped disconsolately across the road, brushed through the bead curtains, and entered.

A young and pretty girl greeted them smilingly.

"Seven *cafés au lait*," said Jan, "and a bowl of milk."

They sat near the entrance at a marble-topped table. The only other occupants were a very old longshoreman and two neatly dressed civilians at an opposite table. The latter looked up swiftly as the seven came in and as quickly glanced away.

"Well, what are we going to do?" said Karel.

"I think we're finished," said Ludva.

"If you talk like that," rebuked Josef, "you will be."

"Then you suggest something," said Ludva.

The coffee was brought in by the girl who had welcomed them, helped by two younger girls. While the cups were being set round the table the men learned that the three girls were sisters, that their mother ran the café and that their father was in the French Navy and they hadn't had any news of him for over three months. The girls were pleased to tell their troubles to the sympathetic young airmen, and anxious, in their turn, to show their sympathy for men in the uniform of their country's Air Force.

The men relaxed in the pleasant atmosphere, but as soon as the girls had left their table they resumed their anxious conversation.

"Well," said Karel, "the boats have all sailed."

"The next best thing's an airplane," said Joska. "After all, we know something about the job. We're all flying crew."

"There must be an airdrome somewhere near," said Karel.

"It's a good suggestion," said Vlasta. Then he leaned across the table. "Don't look round," he said in a low voice, "but the two civilians over there seem too interested in us."

"I think they're police," said Gustav. "I've been watching them."

"And probably in German pay," said Josef.

"Look out," said Jan. "One of them's coming over."

The stouter of the two was crossing toward them. His companion, still seated, began to beat a tattoo on the table top.

"Excuse me, gentlemen," said the stout man politely, "but may I have a word with you?"

"By all means, Monsieur," said Vlasta. "Sit down."

"I gather that you are members of the French Air Force," the stout man continued, "and that you understand how to fly airplanes."

"That is so," said Vlasta.

"That is very interesting," said the other.

"Forgive my intrusion," said Jan, "but why do you ask? We are private individuals and our business is private."

The stout man smiled. "I am going too fast." His brow darkened. "You do not suspect us of being police?"

"Forgive us," said Vlasta, "but it's possible, isn't it?"

"I hate the Germans," said the stout man emphatically. He beckoned across to the other table. "Come here," he called to his companion.

The tall, dark man sauntered over.

"Are you in difficulties already, Henri?" he said smiling.

"No, Charles," cried the stout man. "No, no. But they think we are police in the pay of the Germans."

"Mon Dieu!" said Charles. "Police!"

He sat himself down with an arm over the back of a chair.

"I hate the Boche," said the stout man. "They were never to be trusted. I hate the sight and smell of them."

He struck the table so that the cups rattled in their saucers.

His companion smiled at them, "He'd never make a pilot, would he?" he said. "Much too heavy-handed. Is that your dog?"

"Yes," said Jan, beginning to feel reassured. "He's mine all right."

The man named Charles held out his hand.

"Say 'how-do-you-do,' " said Jan.

Antis raised a paw.

"Charming! Intelligent!" And he smiled his delightful smile again. Then the smile gave way to a look both shrewd and keen. He tapped the stout man on the shoulder.

"Apply yourself, Henri," he said. "Produce your credentials as I now produce mine. Then we can talk business."

He drew a sheaf of papers from his pocket.

"I am Charles le Fèvre and my friend is Henri Fournier. We are both good Frenchmen and abhor the action taken by the men of Vichy, who are traitors to their country. I assure you, the actions of Marshal Pétain are by no means upheld in certain diplomatic circles, nor by all high-ranking officers of the French Forces.

"We have a proposition to lay before you, gentlemen. Will one of you speak for you all? A committee of one works quickest."

"Vlasta's our spokesman," said Jan, and the others agreed in a chorus.

"Then M. Fournier and I will lay our proposition before your friend, Vlasta," said Charles le Fèvre. "And when he has heard what we have to say he can return to you and you can discuss it together. Is that agreeable, gentlemen?"

They agreed unanimously.

Vlasta crossed with the two Frenchmen to their original table. Karel clapped Ludva on the back. "Our luck's on the turn," he said. "No firing squad for the likes of us. Even the dog knows it. Look how his tail's signaling! Come here, you rascal, and tell me what you know."

Then Vlasta was back at their table, his face serious.

"Well?" said Karel.

"I think they are genuine," Vlasta said. "Their identification papers seem to be in order. I think it's a chance we've got to take. But we'll watch out for any tricks."

"Go on," urged Karel. "Go on. Don't keep us in suspense."

"This is the setup," said Vlasta. "There are quite a few bigwigs who don't agree with Pétain. They want to fight on from Algiers. Our friends here tell me the rest of their party are gathered together on an airdrome near Montpellier. They've got two aircraft but only one crew—the other panicked at the last minute. They want us to fly the second aircraft out of this country for them. I have said that we'll all go to Montpellier with them and see what the aircraft are like. The final plans for getting out of France will be discussed when we reach Montpellier. We start in an hour's time. When Fournier and Le Fèvre leave this café we're to follow them at a distance and not attract attention. It's no good hanging on here. There will be no more convoys. I think it's a chance we've got to take, so I've accepted the offer as far as it goes. But watch out for any funny business. I hope I've done right."

"You've done magnificently," said Jan.

"And so say all of us!" said Karel. "What about it, Antis, you ill-begotten mongrel, you approve of that, don't you?"

And Antis, sensing excitement, began to bark.

The men made their farewells to the girls in a mood of

optimism very different from their feelings on arrival at the café. The oldest girl gave Jan a lock of her hair for luck.

4

As Le Fèvre drove the big car slowly across the immense meadow choked with thistle and weeds, Jan kept thinking of Vlasta's warning. This deserted place would indeed make an excellent trap. Even Karel had fallen silent.

The house at the far side was heavily shuttered. They drew up before the neglected garden, its paths and margins obliterated by weeds. No sound at all came from the house as Le Fèvre led them around to the back.

There in the fading light they saw two obsolescent, camouflaged bombers standing among the trees. One was a Bloch 200, but the other was an Amiot 143, a plane in which they had all flown many hours.

"Come and have a look," said Le Fèvre. "We shall be interested to hear your views."

"I think I can speak for all of us," said Vlasta immediately, "if the Amiot's serviceable, we can fly it."

"Our three mechanics say that both airplanes can be made airworthy within six hours," said Le Fèvre.

"Very well," said Vlasta, "other things being equal, the deal's on."

"Excellent," said Le Fèvre. "Now, if you will follow me, gentlemen?"

He led them into the house, through a dark hall crowded with luggage, and then into a large room at the back. Eleven men were present, divided into two groups. Jan could tell that the argumentative, gesticulating group were civilians and those at a table poring over maps were the military. They were clearly in a state of dissension. Le Fèvre introduced the seven to everyone, and then took them over to the corner to meet the four young men wearing the uniform of the French Air Force. They were the other crew.

Le Fèvre turned to Vlasta. "These people flew both aircraft in yesterday afternoon. The pilot is a Pole, but the rest are French. Will you please decide among yourselves which airplane you will fly when we make up our minds which route we shall take?"

The airmen had no trouble at all in making their decision, since the Polish pilot and his crew were as accustomed to Blochs as the Czech men were to Amiots. But the discussion of the route in the other part of the room grew lengthier and more heated until finally the tallest member of the military group, who was addressed as "Colonel," asked Vlasta to give his opinion.

A small and pompous gentleman had no hesitation in approaching Vlasta at once.

"It is, of course, understood," he said, extending his chest like a pouter-pigeon, "that you are flying direct to Gibraltar. That is the route I—that is, we—have chosen."

"Not in the Amiot, which is the aircraft we will fly," said Vlasta.

"What in the world do you mean?"

"Nobody would fly an Amiot that distance without refueling, sir," said Vlasta, "so the only course is to stop at Algiers."

"Algiers? I've never heard such a thing in my life," said the little man.

The Colonel came over to Vlasta. "Explain your difficulty," he said. There was a twinkle in his eye. "Perhaps as a mere soldier, I can understand!"

"It is six hundred and eighty miles to Gib, sir, by your map, which I've looked at," said Vlasta. "And sixty miles to avoid flying over Spain. Which is getting beyond the range of the Amiot with an excess load. But if we lob down at Algiers, which is four hundred and eighty and is just possible with an extra tank, we can refuel and make Gib from there. It's simple arithmetic, sir."

"Very well," agreed the Colonel. "If that's your deci-

sion, then I will see that those traveling in the Amiot agree
to it."

"Thank you, sir."

"What about the other aircraft?"

"That's not my concern, sir. I wouldn't risk it, but it's
up to them. And there's one more point, sir."

"Go on," said the Colonel, "I respect your views."

"Not all that luggage in the passage, sir," said Vlasta.
"Overloaded as we shall be, I am not taking more than a
hundred and fifty pounds per head."

Finally all differences were resolved. The Bloch would
fly direct to Gibraltar, but the Amiot, with the crew of
seven Czechs, three civilians, and one officer as passengers, would break the journey at Algiers.

An hour before midnight the crews of both aircraft,
with the three mechanics, withdrew to service their aircraft during the precious hours before dawn.

When dawn came on June 30 both aircraft took off
successfully, setting course for the Mediterranean, the
Bloch leading. As they crossed the coast of France they
parted company, the leading aircraft altering course several degrees to the southwest. The Amiot flew directly south
with nine-tenths cloud cover. The passengers were uncom-
fortably crowded, but everyone's spirits were high. After
three hours Ludva put the Amiot's nose down to pick up
the predetermined landmark of the Balearic Islands and
check their position. Their navigation had been admirable. They were dead on course.

5

Jan, from his gun turret with his dog lying at his feet,
could see Majorca to starboard, jeweled on an ocean of
silver. The island was edged with a delicate tracery of
white where the sea rippled along the shore and against
the cliffs. On the port beam nothing moved on the peace-

ful water, but he could see now, almost directly beneath them, two ships steaming in line. He had a momentary impression of a third ship, when a small black cloud suddenly attracted his attention. Within the instant the first sinister black puff was followed by another and another. At the same time the Amiot started to bank and climb as the pilot took evasive action and the explosions shook the air. The vessels beneath were hostile and opening fire on them.

Ludva, weaving desperately, was climbing toward the protective cloud, as the shrapnel burst still nearer, and the Amiot shuddered and shook. Whoever was below had clearly been ready for them. Then the friendly cloud was floating past Jan's turret and he knew that they were unobserved from below. It had been a near thing, he told himself. They had been caught napping.

He wondered, not without malice, how their civilian passengers were, so he leaned down out of the turret to listen. The consensus of opinion seemed to be that their enemy was Italian. Antis, lying peacefully at his feet, had shown no more concern than any dog dozing on a rug by a fireside.

Then, astonishingly, they were once again bathed in brilliant sunshine. They had inadvertently come out of a cloud and were in full view of those waiting below.

Almost at once a series of explosions rocked the Amiot. There was a clattering on his right, and the port engine began to cough and splutter. An ominous trail of oily black smoke started to race past his turret. The aircraft hung poised for a second and then, its nose plunging downward, went into a spiral spin towards the sea. Jan fell heavily on his shoulder and Antis was flung to the roof. The crew and passengers were struggling in a wild confusion of arms and legs and baggage while Ludva fought to keep the aircraft under control.

They came out of the spin at five hundred feet, and miraculously Ludva checked the dive at fifty feet and flattened out into a shallow glide. Then in a great cloud of spray the Amiot plunged into the sea.

The hurricane roar and whistling of air suddenly stopped. It was silent, but for the lapping of the water against the sides of the aircraft. Jan grabbed Antis by the collar and forced his way out through the nearest hatch. The others were emerging one by one. No one, beyond a few bruises, appeared in the least hurt. Jan could see Josef and Vlasta swimming in the heavy swell and three of their passengers clinging to the fuselage. Ludva and the Army officer were hauling themselves hand over hand towards the starboard wing.

The Amiot refused to sink for a time. She remained for fully five minutes with her tail cocked up like a duck about to dive. Joska and Karel dismantled the guns from the outside. Vlasta climbed through the turret to salvage all belongings within reach.

Jan crawled onto the tilting wing, hauling Antis by the collar. Antis frantically struggled to find a grip on the taut and slippery surface. When at last man and dog were perched on the wing tip both were exhausted. Antis in his panic had swallowed mouthfuls of water and lay inert, a dead weight across Jan's arm. The Amiot gave a shudder and at last began to subside.

Clinging desperately to his perch, Jan took stock of the situation. Across the sunlit water he could see the three ships that he had viewed from above. There were two large cargo vessels and an Italian cruiser. One of the cargo vessels was lowering a boat. The others were proceeding at half speed. Within minutes, they were all aboard the merchantman's longboat. A quarter of an hour later they were aboard the vessel itself, disarmed and under guard, with mugs of hot coffee in their hands before they stripped off their clothes to dry them.

"Of all the bloody luck," Vlasta said to Jan, "and we were doing so well."

Antis shook himself for the hundredth time. One of the Italian sailors began to fondle him. He was a tall, handsome fellow, though marred by an ugly scar running across his forehead. Like the rest of the crew, he had displayed no enmity, but rather a friendly curiosity. He

now made some comment to a fellow seaman, who pointed at Jan and shrugged his shoulders. The guard, who had
assumed an officially correct attitude of indifference towards his charges, growled an order to the onlookers and
they began to disperse.

"What the hell's going to happen to us?" said Ludva.

"Prisoners of war," said Vlasta bitterly, "*Italian* prisoners of war—we hope!"

"If they hand us over to the Germans————" cried
Karel. And stopped short at the dark thoughts that instantly filled not only his own mind.

Towards evening three of the crew brought food and
blankets. The naval guard made no attempt to interfere,
but turned his back while the prisoners ate. When they
had spread out their blankets on deck and were preparing
for a night under the stars, the young sailor with the scar
across his forehead reappeared. He leaned against a ventilator, his eyes intent on Antis a dozen paces away. Jan,
mind and body worn with the stress of the day, turned on
his side. The deck made a hard bed, but he supposed the
bottom of the Mediterranean would have been worse.

He dozed, dimly aware of the watcher by the ventilator
and the dog by his side. Vexation rose within him, but he
quelled it with the thought that far more momentous
questions were to be faced. What if the Italian authorities
decided to hand them over to the Germans? He was
reassuring himself that such a speculation had no reason-
able grounds, when he heard half a dozen rapid footsteps
and a low growl.

He sat up, throwing the blanket from him. The Italian
seaman, with Antis struggling in his arms, was striding
away across the deck.

Jan leaped up and caught the fellow by the shoulder.

"That's my dog," said Jan.

Several of the figures near him stirred, and the guard
picked up the rifle beside him and took a step forward.
The young seaman faced about. He was grinning all over
his face.

"Give me my dog," said Jan furiously, and stretched

out his hand. The Italian laughed and shook him off, hugging Antis to his chest. The guard drew level with the two of them.

"Tell him to give me back my property," said Jan, shaking with indignation.

Seaman and guard exchanged a dozen words. The guard shrugged his shoulders, and the former turned on his heel, and with Antis in his arms, disappeared around the ventilator. The guard raised his rifle, barring Jan's way. He motioned him back towards his blanket.

"Please," said Jan, controlling himself, "the dog is a most valued possession. If you only knew his story————"

The guard rapped out an unintelligible order. Jan pointed wildly in the direction that the young Italian had taken. The guard drew the butt of his rifle threateningly back on his shoulder.

"Damn and blast you!" cried Jan, and sank down on his blanket, his head in his hands.

For several moments the guard stood menacingly over him, but for all Jan cared he could have been a thousand miles away. At length the guard returned to his bollard and took out his pipe and began to smoke. But Jan remained in the same position of despair on his makeshift bed.

The sultry night dragged slowly by. From time to time a ship's bell rang, and once when a door opened Jan could hear voices and laughter. The guard changed. On either side of him Jan could see the dark shapes of his comrades. Once, to his dismay and embarrassment, he heard the sound of weeping. He was not alone with sorrow.

He had lost Antis. That young brute had borne him away, loot from a defenseless prisoner. He would never see his dog again.

It was a loss not to be replaced. They had begun to grow together. Jan had heard before of the mystic bond between an animal and a human being that even the barrier of the spoken word could not prevent. And that young brute of a sailor had stolen his beloved dog. Now he realized the value of all he had found and lost. He bea his temples with the palms of his hands. He wished he were dead.

At midnight a sound penetrated the frozen core of his mind, which for hours had relinquished thought. He shifted his position, not at all surprised that his legs were stiff with cramp and that his body ached with cold. He could see the figure of the guard, hunched on the bollard. The man suddenly stirred and looked over his shoulder.

Then down the length of the deck, pattering in a tattoo that brought Jan to his feet, came the sound of a dog scampering wildly along the resounding planks.

"Antis!" cried Jan.

He stood up with outstretched arms, and the dog leapt into them.

The guard left his bollard, imperiously waving aside the sailor with the scar on his forehead, who came pelting down the deck in bare feet. He took little notice of that other's babbling oaths, fascinated by the spectacle of the man and the dog clasped as one together. He stood with his head on one side, nodding and approving. Only when the sailor shook his fist in his face did he slam the brass-shod rifle butt on to the deck, missing the other's toe by a quarter of an inch, so that he turned and fled.

The guard said to Jan in broken Provençal patois:

"Nice dog. Very nice dog. He belongs to you and no mistake."

"No mistake at all," cried Jan triumphantly.

"I understand," said the guard.

Order restored, he returned to his seat on the bollard.

Under their blanket Antis lay by Jan's side, the man's right arm clasped fast around his dog. The first indication of approaching fog was wreathing in spirals across the affrail as the stars began to fade.

6

In the dense fog at dawn, the ship's decks rattled with emergency. Bells rang, and seamen scurried about prying open hatch covers and uncovering lifeboats.

The disconsolate group of fellow prisoners were huddled together aft of the bridge. Ludva was just remarking, "There's a panic on. People running about when they should be walking," when the lookout began to shout. There was a sudden ringing of bells and orders shouted through a megaphone. The sailors looked up with scared faces.

Then, without warning, two hundred yards to starboard a vast dark shape loomed through the fog. For a moment as the haze parted all of them saw the formidable outline of a battleship. Jan could see the guns of her broadside imperceptibly dipping to correct the range.

"She's a French cruiser," cried Vlasta.

"And there's another just behind her," shouted Joska.

The fog lifted again and a ray of sunshine broke through revealing the tapering steel foremast of the second vessel. At the peak fluttered the Union Jack.

"She's British!" shouted Jan. "She's————"

And then the deafening crash of the first broadside swept the words from his lips.

It was all over before it began. The Italian convoy, caught by surprise, went to the bottom in a matter of minutes. Panic and confusion reigned supreme. The vessel immediately took a heavy list to port. Kit bags and luggage skidded across the sloping deck. Within seconds the ship was on fire from stem to stern. The air was filled with splinters, smoke, and flying glass. The screams of the wounded could be heard above the uproar of the cannonade. Jan picked himself up with Antis in his arms. Ludva leaped for the rail as the merchantman heeled over.

"Come on!" he shouted, and went over the side.

Jan, his arms around the dog, followed suit. He saw the water rushing up to meet him and then he struck the surface flat and, with Antis still gripped in his arms, went down into the green darkness.

He regained the surface with lungs that threatened to burst. The dog was struggling wildly in his grasp. All around the sea was black with floating oil. It clung to his hair, his mouth, and his nostrils, like a film of black treacle. A flame at the edge of each black pool would suddenly melt into its neighbor to form one sheet of leaping fire. Then the flames would mount still higher. Over all rolled a black billowing smoke that blotted out the sky. The dog slipped from Jan's arms.

All around the sea was on fire. The smoke curled into his nostrils and his hair caught fire. He ducked his head and shoulders and came up on the edge of fire that licked his hands, webbed, glutinous, and dripping with oil. He shouted:

"Antis! Antis!"

The smoke came down and stung his eyes. He attempted to wipe them clear, but the oil coagulated across his cheekbones and mouth. He choked and coughed and vomited black filth. On every side he could hear men screaming. He could see nothing. He knew that he was very likely about to die.

Then suddenly the smoke was whisked head high, caught in an updraft. He sucked a gust of fresh air into his lungs. He could see five yards ahead, and open water on his left. He dashed black froth from his lips.

He found Antis by his side, thrashing the surface with frantic paws.

"Swim, boy, swim!" he shouted.

The dog plunged towards him and climbed onto his back. They both went down gasping. Then they were up again and a crate was drifting past. Jan grabbed the crate and steadied it for the dog to climb up on it. The oil-saturated forepaws slipped, missed their hold. The crate slid from Jan's fingers as the dog tore at his back, mounted again, and forced him under. When they came up for the second time it was in the midst of wreckage. A plank floated out of the smoke. Jan flung his arm over it, flung the other around his dog. He began to yell violent oaths, dripping, drowning in slime.

To his left he thought he saw, through eyes with cluttered lids, a patch of sunlight and calm, shining water. He drove dog and plank towards it as it disappeared.

There were voices shouting in a strange tongue. He shouted back as the mountain of smoke collapsed. He could hear oars. A solid substance struck the plank. It slipped from his oily fingers.

Then his hand struck an oar and a voice shouted:

"Here's another."

He had no idea what was being said. He flung his arms out wildly and the dog slid from his side.

"Up you come, mate. . . . Easy now. . . . Easy now. . . . Get hold of the life line, you stupid bastard . . . up you come . . ."

How could he understand when they were talking gibberish? Why couldn't they talk sense? Then there were hands under his armpits, heaving, lifting. They were breaking his ribs as they hauled him over the gunwale. Why rescue a man if they'd got to stove in his ribs?

Then he was lying across a thwart of the whaler, belching, spewing.

"Take it easy, mate. . . . Cor, strike a light, look at the bloody pooch. . . . Cough it up, mate. Empty your guts. . . . Come on, Fido, good dog, cough your heart up, mate. . . . Fancy picking a dog up among the ice-cream boys—Sick it up, Fido . . ."

7

They arrived at Gibraltar the following morning, seven Czech airmen, one French Army officer, three civilians, and a dog. The Royal Navy handed the Czechs and the dog over to the Royal Air Force, who had been previously signaled to expect them. They were the sole survivors of the party that had set out from Montpellier at dawn, two days previously. The Bloch had crashed within sight of Gibraltar. Fuel had given out.

chapter iv   *"All Baggage Safely Disembarked"*

1

They were in excellent spirits. They were bound for England. The grimy, rusty collier *Northman* lay a hundred yards off the jetty. To their eyes she was as lovely a ship as ever graced the sea.

At Gibraltar the Royal Air Force had given them a change of clothes and plenty to eat. The story of their escape from France and rescue from the Mediterranean twice in twenty-four hours had gone the rounds. The Navy had washed them down, including the dog, revived them, looked after them, and passed them over to the Air Force, with very little fuss and a degree of nonchalance. They had been impressed with the smooth efficiency.

There was a gangway from the jetty up to the ferry-boat that was to put them aboard the *Northman,* and all the morning she had been ferrying across refugees of all kinds and classes. Now they went up the gangway in single file, Vlasta first, Antis last. At the head of the gangway stood a British Military Policeman and a French sailor, checking names and documents. The sun was shining, the day warm.

Jan was giving thanks, as he went along the gangway, for their miraculous luck. They were all together after the last, incredible twenty-four hours, and they were going to England as they had hoped. Nothing could go wrong now.

But, it seemed, something could. The French sailor examined his papers and handed them back.

"In order. But whose is the dog?"

"Mine," said Jan.

"Sorry," said the sailor. "No dogs allowed on board. We've already had to stop a Colonel. But you'll find a good home for him ashore easily. You've got plenty of time to look around. Yes? Next please?"

"Take my kit," said Jan to Joska. "I'll follow later."

He went down to the quay. He waved to Vlasta and Karel in the ferryboat as it departed. Joska was at their side, explaining. All three waved back to him.

He sat down on a pile of wood to think. He knew that if Antis could not get on board, then neither would he. Separation was an impossibility. But it was some little time and a cup of coffee later before his eye fell on the old ship's bucket on the wharf and the solution came to him.

"We'll wait until dusk," he said to Antis. The dog looked up and wagged his tail.

"Anyone would think you understood," said Jan. "I hope to God you will when the time comes."

They went into the neighboring canteen and ate supper. When they came out at dusk, Jan prayed that the training he had given Antis would survive the test ahead. He was still a very young dog. But their future depended on it.

He could see the *Northman* against the sunset and hear voices across the water. Nobody was about. He fetched the bucket and lifted Antis into it. The dog sat, his forepaws resting on the rim. Jan caressed his ears and patted him.

"Good lad," he said.

Then he raised his finger and spoke in a special tone that Antis knew well.

"Wait till I call," said Jan. *"Wait."*

He lowered the bucket to the level of the water and tied its rope to an iron ring. Then he strode to the ferry.

The *Northman* was crowded with over a hundred refugees from nearly every country in Europe. It seemed as though a huge party were in progress. But over it all, Jan heard Karel's voice as soon as he stepped on board, and he followed the sound.

Karel was surrounded by twelve more Czechs he had

found on board, nearly all of the Czech Air Force. He was telling them the story of the flight from Montpellier. But Joska came over to Jan and listened to the Antis plan. He called to the others to gather around.

"We've got to find a place to hide the dog on board," said Karel. He struck his forehead with his palms. "Well, you just get him here, and we'll do the rest."

"If I could only find a ladder," said Jan.

"They are using one for bathing over the stern," Joska said.

As Jan shouldered his way through the crowd he wondered how they would find room to sleep that night. But they were chattering too happily for thoughts of sleep, and Jan realized how free from danger and death they felt, setting off for England, the land of the free. Then he remembered that if Antis failed to answer his signal, he himself might never see England.

When he found the ladder at the stern and climbed down to the last rung over the water, it was dark. He put the hollow of his cupped hand to his mouth and whistled.

A minute passed. It was very quiet. Jan whistled again. This time he thought he heard a faint clank and a splash, but couldn't be sure. He could see the familiar shape of Joska's head leaning over the rail above him. Then he heard the dog. He called softly.

"Here, boy. Here."

Antis, swimming strongly, came down the length of the ship. In half a minute Jan could see his dark head between the ripples. Then he leant out and grasped the dog's collar. Together they struggled up the first few rungs of the ladder as Joska came down to meet them.

"The chaps are all ready for you," he whispered. "Up you go."

They went up hand over hand and clambered over the rail.

"Quick," said Karel. "Wrap him in this."

He handed over his greatcoat. The other five closed round them. In a solid phalanx they moved across the deck. The dog, almost completely enveloped in the coat, never stirred. A sailor stood aside to let them pass.

"Sorting yourselves out, mates?" he said. "That's the ticket. What a caper!"

Understanding nothing of what he said, they nodded, grinned, and marched on. Nobody followed them.

"Here," said Karel. "The best we can do. Down you go."

They stood shoulder to shoulder round the edge of the open manhole. It yawned as black and deep as the Pit itself.

"There's a ladder," said Karel. "After all our trouble don't break your neck. Take my torch."

By the time they reached the bottom Jan had lost count of the rungs. Standing with Antis beside him in the pitch dark hold, he could see far above him the faint shape of the manhole opening. He switched on the torch and looked around him.

He was standing in a small compartment of the after hold. He supposed that the propeller shafts ran beneath him. It was deathly quiet now, but later the tumult and vibration would become unbearable. Nevertheless, he could see that Karel and the rest had solved the immediate problem.

The place was thick with coal dust. He could see the motes floating across the beam of the torch. Antis sneezed and shook himself.

"There's your bed," said Jan.

Karel had thought of everything. There was one bed for the man and one for the dog. They had all realized that Jan would never leave Antis. This was the quality of their friendship. He knew that it would never fail.

Three days later, twenty-eight ships in convoy, with four destroyers of the Royal Navy in escort, steamed out of Gibraltar harbor bound for England.

2

There seemed to be no end to contriving. He sat in the ship's boat with his six friends and twenty-four refugees. The second day out of port, *Northman's* engines had broken down, and every one aboard had been ordered to transfer to the armed merchantman *Neuralia,* which they were now running alongside. It was a ticklish business fraught with danger. His hand was on his kit bag and there it would remain till the transfer was complete.

Joska, who with the others had included his share of Jan's belongings in their own baggage, said:

"He's pretty quiet. I suppose he's all right?"

He cast a critical eye at Jan's kit bag.

"Good as gold," affirmed Jan.

"When we get him aboard we'll find another place all right. Don't you worry."

"He's being a damn nuisance to you all," said Jan.

"He's one of us," said Joska. "We stick together, don't we?"

The boat bumped alongside the foot of the ladder.

"We'll keep near you," said Joska. "You go in the middle."

They mounted the ladder one by one. Two naval officers, a petty officer, and a Czech interpreter awaited them on the quarter deck. Sudden movement in his kit bag induced Jan to tighten his grip.

"Come along," ordered the interpreter. "Please to hurry."

The kit bag under Jan's arm became convulsed. He hurriedly took the last step to the deck and the neck cord slipped from his finger as the interpreter momentarily turned his head.

Josef, half a dozen paces away, said:

"Oh, my God! He's got out!"

Antis, his head encircled in the neck of the kit bag like a ruff, stared into the astonished face of the Officer of the Watch.

The game was up. Jan knew what they would order him to do. And if he refused, they themselves would drop his dog over the side, and that would be an end of it. He stood at the head of the ladder and gaped speechless. Then Joska was babbling in Czechoslovakian, attempting to plead with the interpreter.

"Hullo," said the Officer of the Watch. "A stowaway!" He was smiling all over his boyish face. "Let the poor beggar out," he said. "You'll have him suffocating."

He jerked the cord of the kit bag free. Antis dropped on all fours on the spotless deck and shook himself. A cloud of coal dust arose around him like a satanic halo.

"Get him below before the 'old man' sees what you've done to his deck," said the Officer of the Watch to Jan.

"Pass along," said the interpreter. "Please to hurry."

Jan moved along the deck in a daze, with Antis trotting behind him.

"Third-class berths up forward," said the petty officer as they passed. "That's a nice dog you've got. Where's he been—in the stokehole?"

"And give him a bath before he comes on deck again," called the Officer of the Watch. Then the remainder of the boatload were crowding on to the deck. Josef had gone forward to explore and was now returning.

"Come and see for yourselves," cried Josef. "Real bunks and clean blankets and washbowls in the cabins. It's like heaven."

3

There were forty-eight hours to go. By this time tomorrow they would be steaming up the Mersey. It seemed too good to be true, Jan told himself, as the last few days had been too good to last.

Vlasta put his head round the cabin door.

"All owners of pets to report to the captain's cabin," he said. "The interpreter asked me to pass it on. That's all I know."

Over a dozen passengers waited outside the cabin. A Lieutenant R.N.R. acted as the captain's spokesman. His instructions were brief. All animals were to be handed over to the ship's authorities, who would arrange for quarantine for six months, provided the kennel fees were duly paid.

A Czech soldier, who possessed a handsome mastiff, asked what the outcome might be if an owner was penniless. He was told that if anyone could not afford the fees his dog would be painlessly destroyed. It was the British Ministry of Agriculture's regulation.

Jan had only a few francs left and a ten-shilling note provided by R.A.F. welfare at Gibraltar. He returned to his friends inconsolable. He could see no solution to this major problem.

To defy the law was to risk imprisonment or deportation. The total funds that all seven could provide would scarcely last for three weeks' fees.

Then Joska spoke:

"Antis was the Squadron's dog, and we're all that's left of the Squadron. We can't desert him any more than we could desert one another."

Everyone agreed.

"But *how?*" said Jan. "In the name of God, *how?*"

"There's a pile of luggage down below under a tarpaulin," said Karel darkly, "with a very large crate right in the center. If I know our officer no awkward questions will be asked. So choose a time when the crew are busy. Anyway, we could be sorting out our belongings if they ask what we're about."

"And what are we about?" asked Joska.

"We take out the big case and put it on the edge of the rest of the baggage. Then we rearrange the stuff so that a tunnel leads to the space in the center. And that for the next forty-eight hours will be Antis' home."

"Brilliant," said Vlasta. "If our officer says it's all right it will be all right with the Navy. They've got enough on their hands, anyway. I'll have a word with the officer. If anyone gets too inquisitive play dumb. There's always the language difficulty."

The following day an inspection of quarters took place with a view to checking all animals aboard. There was only one missing, a young Alsatian dog with a distinctive black marking down his spine.

Jan was called before two naval officers. He found it unfortunate that they were near the luggage whose rearrangement had aroused no comment so far. But no sign came from the dog in his den.

"You've not handed over your dog."

"I haven't seen him for several hours, sir," said Jan.

"You know this is a serious offense?"

"I'm not committing an offense, sir," said Jan. "I just haven't seen the dog."

"Very well. But don't tell us you didn't realize the penalty."

They searched the ship but they found no dog. At five o'clock they gave up. At six o'clock Vlasta told Jan that Lieut. Josef Ocelka, who had arrived to meet the Czech detachment aboard H.M.S. *Neuralia,* had appointed Jan, himself, and Joska to be in charge of the embarkation of all baggage belonging to the detachment.

"All baggage," said Vlasta, looking Jan plumb in the eye, "to be safely disembarked."

"I understand," said Jan.

"Make sure you do," said Vlasta.

4

It was the evening of July 12, 1940. On H.M.S. *Neuralia* the fifty Czechs paraded amidship with their small kit, preparatory to disembarkation. Their luggage was slung on to the dockside and into the waiting lorries under the watchful eyes of Jan and Joska. But Antis, repeating the ruse that had nearly succeeded before, was safe in Jan's kit bag.

Within the hour the contingent were paraded on the main departure platform of Liverpool Central Station. The airmen's kit bags were piled in a loose heap on the platform. That labeled "R. V. Bozdech" rested on top.

Eight Military Policemen and half a dozen civilian police officers patrolled the station.

Three minutes before the train for Cholmondeley steamed in, the butt of a rifle inadvertently struck the kit bag labeled "R. V. Bozdech." A loud and penetrating yelp issued from the kit bag.

Immediately all policemen began to close in for the kill. The personnel of the Czech detachment, as always eager to be of assistance, started to search among their baggage, heaving it from side to side and throwing from hand to hand at great speed one special kit bag until it was well clear of the suspected area. Nevertheless, the police would never have abandoned the hunt had it not been for the ready wit of Vaclav Stetka, who slapped a hand to his own calf while emitting a piercing likeness to a canine yelp.

The Military Police, declaring that "No bloody foreigner was going to take the Mickey out of them!" gave up the search.

A quarter of an hour later the eight comrades were on their way to their first camp in the United Kingdom.

I

787641 A.C.2 R. V. (Jan) Bozdech sat in his quarters at Royal Air Force Station, Duxford, studying *Fundamental English.* It had been a quiet night, free from enemy activity. Antis lay at his feet, hunting rabbits in his sleep. Dog and man, grown closer together than ever, had now been in England just under two months.

It seemed to Jan that a great deal had happened in a remarkably short space of time. He laid down his book and lit a cigarette. It was about time he took a breather from learning this devilish language, which spelled words one way and pronounced them another. The dog, his four legs working, yelped in his sleep. Jan touched him lightly with his toe.

"You make too much noise," he said with a smile.

Antis thumped the floor with an appreciative tail and immediately went to sleep again. Jan let his mind wander back over the last six weeks.

They had arrived at Cholmondeley on that July midnight in pouring rain, in many ways a dismal introduction to the stalwart island that had for so long now colored his imagination. But the following sunny morning he had looked out of the tent and marveled at the lush green meadows, the splendid grove of chestnut trees, and the nearby brook. His spirits had risen at once and he had raced down to the stream with the rest of them to wash. After that wash he had wandered through the tented lines and had greeted old friends with extravagant enthusiasm; and had seen fathers find their sons and sons, brothers, so that all their world of exiles seemed akin.

They had stayed eighteen days at Cholmondeley. Jan and his dog had gone for long walks in a rabbit-infested dog's paradise. At night Antis had made his regular bedtime inspection, never retiring to his own blanket till he had nosed each of his friends' faces to satisfy himself that all were present.

In the third week of July the President of Czechoslovakia, Dr. Eduard Beneš, had paid them a visit, and all the personnel at the camp had paraded. A week later on July 30, 1940, the seven friends, with Antis at their head, had moved to the Czech Air Force Depot at R.A.F. Station, Cosford, near Wolverhampton, with twenty-nine other airmen.

Jan wondered if he would ever forget the Fulton Block which had housed them at Cosford. It was shaped in the form of a capital "H," could contain a thousand airmen, and possessed four main doors of entry. It was possible for the uninitiated to become hopelessly lost within seconds. Airmen seeking the mess arrived in the latrines, those longing for their bed found themselves back in the main porch.

Legend went that the Fulton Block had been so diabolically designed to keep apart squadrons of pugnacious Boy Apprentices at night. The story appealed to the exiles as a fine example of fighting spirit.

At Cosford, Jan had found time to train his dog. Realizing that he would be spending much of his life in the air while Antis remained alone at the base, he concentrated on instilling implicit obedience.

He was no more experienced than the next man in the training of an animal, but he proceeded by demanding of him nothing that was impractical nor beyond him at each stage of development and taking him gradually forward step by step. If the intention were walking a narrow plank or climbing a ladder or jumping an obstruction, he first made sure that the task could be performed without the dog's hurting himself. More experienced friends would look askance at the method of treating the animal as a fellow human, whispering encouragement and reassurance into his ear and reproving failure in a similar fashion. But the method worked, principally through infinite patience and infinite love on both sides.

At Cosford, the dog was trained to sit in a spot precisely selected until ordered to move. For all performances the reward or punishment was identical. A long walk in the countryside where rabbits abounded was the height of Antis' pleasure; to be ignored and then peremptorily dismissed, the depths of his chagrin.

In a very short time he had decided upon his own daily round, regardless of his master. At eight-thirty each morning he went to the hospital, where he awaited the arrival of two girls, who invariably kept a bone for him. Then, with his breakfast gnawed clean, he would make his way to the nurses' quarters, till it was time to meet Jan coming out of class. His special friends were three nurses who always petted him and gave him sweets. He spent much time with them, particularly with a dark and pretty young nurse called Pamela.

Eventually, Antis had been instrumental in providing an introduction between Jan and Pamela that had rapidly ripened into friendship. Thereafter there had been long evening walks through the rabbit-infested and peaceful countryside for the three of them.

By the time they left the Fulton Block, Antis could be trusted to remain where he was told until instructed to leave, to obey an order without hesitation, to follow alongside his master faithfully and unobtrusively, and to fetch and carry. One of the more enchanting tricks he had taught himself was to find his master's gloves at the first glorious intimation of a walk and present them to him. It seemed to Jan, even in those early days of a companionship that was to last so long and survive so much, that their escape through France had bound them together with indestructible ties of devotion, trust, and confidence.

On September 9 the second group of Czech personnel at Cosford had been sworn into the Royal Air Force. Postings had followed swiftly. The seven had hoped to be kept together but Joska, Karel, and Gustav were posted to No. 312 (Bomber) Squadron at Honington, and Jan, with Josef and Vaclav Stetka, to No. 312 (Fighter) Squadron at Duxford. Vlasta had been left behind in hospital with a minor complaint.

Jan had now been at Duxford for nearly two weeks. They had proved so far disappointing. The Czechs had been promised Defiants which had not arrived. The three friends, while waiting for their aircraft, had been spending their time in the armory attempting to learn as much as possible of the guns with which the Defiants were armed. The station had been regularly attacked by enemy aircraft ever since their arrival.

Antis, like his master, was no lover of air attacks. It seemed to Jan that the dog's association of aircraft with high explosive must have its origin in those very early days of the Siegfried Line. He could well believe it.

He believed less readily the legend begun by the armorers, with whom Antis spent much of his time. They swore that Antis could detect the presence of enemy aircraft before anyone or anything else could. When the low-level, sneak enemy raids would escape defense detection, Antis' symptoms would warn the armorers, who could take cover in time.

Only this very morning, a Dornier had stolen up to the perimeter of the airfield unannounced by sirens. The armorers declared that if Antis had not shown alarm, they would not have reached safety. Antis could be unique because of his previous experiences, but Jan could hardly see the possibility of using him officially as a defense officer.

Jan picked up his *Fundamental English*. He saw that Antis had stopped dreaming, and was lying still and tense, with the slightest quivering down his flanks. Softly at first and then more loudly he began to growl.

"What's the matter?" said Jan.

Antis rose to his feet, and stood listening.

"What is it, boy?" said Jan.

The dog turned his head at the sound of his master's voice. Then he began to growl again, his hackles bristling.

"There's nothing about," said Jan, recognizing the symptoms.

Antis trotted over to the door and stood with his nose at the keyhole. It was the procedure when the sirens had sounded. Usually, both would have made their way together to the nearest shelter. But now there could be no possibility of attack. The fog was down thick. No raiders would appear. It was out of the question.

Antis returned from the door and stood by Jan's chair. He whined and placed a paw on his master's knee, demanding attention.

"Don't be a fool," said Jan, not unkindly. "There's nothing there. It's thick fog. Go and lie down."

The dog, rebuffed, padded over to the door again. He raised his head and whimpered. Jan, exasperated, screwed his chair round with his back to him in the gesture of disapproval.

So much for the armorers. Well, everybody made mistakes and when people were living on their nerves they fancied all sorts of things. Stetka, who prided himself on his increasing knowledge of this terrible tongue, had said that the English had a word for it. "Wind up." A funny sort of word.

The dog settled down again, lying outstretched and relaxed along the threshold, muzzle on paws.

"Well, fool," said Jan. "What was all the trouble about?"

Antis thumped the floor with his tail. Jan crossed the room and stroked him.

"You know what's the matter with you?" said Jan. "You've got—now, what the hell is it?—you've got—'wind up.' Come on, let's go and find Josef."

Even inside the building there were traces of fog. The lights down the corridor had a halo round them.

At the end of the passage they met Liska, who worked in the Operations Room. Jan had known him at home, a pleasing, rosy-cheeked young man with spectacles.

"Just come off duty?" said Jan in greeting.

"I am going to bed," said Liska. "It's a twelve-hour watch, you know."

"They work you too hard," said Jan. "It's bad for your nerves. It'll give you wind up."

"Nerves!" said Liska. "I used to be sorry I had bad sight which stopped me from flying, but I should never have the nerve to fly like you people."

"Oh! We're the heroes all right," said Jan, with a grin.

"I wouldn't have been up there tonight," said Liska. "I'll bet the German that came out tonight had your wind up."

"Tonight?" said Jan. "I heard nothing."

"He was very high. We were plotting him just over fifteen miles away before he turned. I think he must have been lost. Good night to you."

"Good night," said Jan.

He stood for some moments in the passage, deep in thought. Then he flicked his fingers towards the dog.

"Tomorrow," promised Jan, "when the fog's cleared, I'll take you for a special walk. We'll try and find some rabbits."

But the following day the Squadron was moved in its entirety to Speke in the Liverpool area.

2

They had been two weeks at Speke. There the Lockheed Aircraft Company of America assembled the aircraft that had been transported in sections across the

Atlantic. This was why camp rumor had it that the airdrome ranked as a secondary target after the Liverpool Docks.

Jan shared a room with Stetka and the interpreter Mirek Cap. Summer was turning to autumn, and still the three Czechs had nothing to fly. Jan, oppressed with "chair-borne" duties in the Orderly Room and his study of *Fundamental English,* was in the depths of depression.

Then one rainy evening Pamela showed up with "seven days' leave and a cousin in the district." Antis danced his delight, but Jan's pleasure was so intense he was speechless.

As they walked through Speke together, an air raid developed over the docks. The distant gunfire was heavy and incessant, the night ribbed with searchlights, the air vibrant with the crump of bombs.

They made their way to Pamela's quarters. Two hours later when the raid quieted down, Jan left to return to camp.

He decided to take the long way back past the railroad station. Antis was still in need of his walk, but in the dim light the drab streets seemed dreary and inhospitable. Jan's temporary elation began to evaporate. People would soon be returning from their shelters at the bottoms of their suburban gardens; but here in the windy street all movement and color had departed. It was a world of the dead. Soon he would reach the dark, forbidding arch of the viaduct.

He stopped to put Antis on the lead. Lorries could sweep out from behind the brick buttresses without any warning, so that pedestrians had to press themselves close to the wall. He stepped over a puddle and passed under the middle of the viaduct. Before he was halfway through he heard voices singing an old Czech drinking song. The next moment the group of airmen clustered around the far end of the archway had recognized him.

"Why, if it isn't the King of the Clerks," cried someone. "What have you done with your mahogany bomber?"

The term referred to his orderly room desk. A joke,

which originating among the armorers, was now wearing a little thin. After all, there was nothing so disheartening as meeting friends gay in liquor when sober oneself, and therefore allowances must be made.

"Oh! our Jan's a good fellow," said Stetka, and clapped Jan on the shoulder.

A spot of rain splashed against Jan's cheek.

"It was a short raid," said one of the armorers. "Has the 'All Clear' sounded?"

"I've not heard it," said Jan. "It's going to rain. I'm getting back to camp."

Antis, in the lead, began to whine.

"What's the matter, boy?" said Jan to his dog.

"He hears something," said an armorer.

"Look at the dog," said Stetka urgently.

Antis was straining at the leash. His whine grew louder and he began to tremble.

"What is it?" Jan repeated.

The dog turned swiftly to his master and slunk to his side. He stood there shivering. A silence fell on the little group. It seemed very dark and cold beneath the archway. Then they heard the rhythmic, undulating beat of the desynchronized engines.

"They're coming back," said Stetka.

The air was trembling with the throb of airscrews.

"They're overhead," said an armorer.

The flare lit the whole area in a scarlet glare. It came down slowly on its parachute, and houses which had been dark shadows in the night became little indigo and pink boxes. The stanchions of the viaduct stood out like spokes of an umbrella against the unearthly glow. A second flare followed and then the eldritch screech of descending bombs.

They flung themselves to the ground as the first bomb exploded. It seemed to Jan that the pavement rose and struck him in the chest. And then the whole "stick" fell as the guns on the perimeter bellowed and clattered. He could feel the outraged air buffet the back of his head and body. All around was the rumble and roar of falling masonry. The gritty smell and taste of dust spread through the rain. Then, incredibly, there was a long silence.

He was alive and he could tell by the quivering form beneath his right arm that Antis lived. At last nearby somebody began to cough and choke. Another rumbling fall of masonry shook the ground. Stetka's voice, perfectly calm and utterly sober, called:

"Is anyone hurt?"

They got to their feet muddy and disheveled. Not one of them had been touched.

"We're all here," said Jan, gasping.

Suddenly voices were everywhere. The silent street had become alive. Dim figures were flitting to and fro. Where there had been a neat row of six houses, now there were only three. The outline of roofs and chimney pots looked as if giant talons had torn across it, leaving a high pile of rubble. A woman ran past, her arms outstretched before her. She slumped and collapsed, as if she'd been shot. Stetka picked her up, held her for a moment, and then propped her against the wall. She collapsed like an empty sack. When he turned to Jan, he was wiping his face free of blood. Somebody in the direction of the rubble gap, which had been a row of villas, began to scream. The nearby screaming continued, rose higher, died away in a long, high-pitched wail of anguish. The sound went through Jan's bowels from navel to spine like the cold thrust of a sword.

"Come on," yelled Stetka. "We've got to get them out."

With Jan at his heels and the armorers trailing behind, he ran out of the arch and into the street like a man demented. A man with blood spurting from the stump of a forearm blundered into Jan.

"Save her!" he shouted. "She's under there. We were having a cup of tea. I've bust my arm. Oh, God! Get her out of there!"

He sat down on the edge of the pavement, plucking at his sleeve and sobbing.

Jan, with Antis bounding before him at the end of his

lead, reached Stetka. He was on his hands and knees, clawing at the debris before him. Jan could see in the light of a torch a hand moving under a pile of bricks. There was a loud rumbling near by as a wall collapsed. The air became thick again. Stetka was flinging bricks and handfuls of mortar over his shoulders. A rescue worker thrust a pick into Jan's hand. Antis, bristling with excitement, was standing by the shattered remains of a kitchen dresser, up to his forepaws in broken china. The screams and moans were now so continuous that Jan scarcely noticed them. Antis, barking, crouched back on his haunches, his head darting forward, then recoiling. The fingers of the buried man were moving, clenching, unclenching.

"Good dog!" said the A.R.P. man. "Get him out. Get him out."

Antis started to dig with frantic forepaws. He was growling deep in his throat.

"Bring the dog over here," said the A.R.P. man. "God! What a shambles."

Jan followed him over a pile of smoking plaster and splintered furniture. The loop of the lead bit into his fingers as the dog plunged forward. He was silent now, his muzzle in the debris. He began to climb the gigantic heap of ruins. All the time Jan was exhorting, urging.

"Seek! Seek! Get them out. Get them out."

Halfway up the heap Antis stopped sniffing. He raised his head and began to bark again. An R.A.F. officer scrambled up beside them. It was Squadron Leader Vasatko, their C.O., down from the camp, his best blue uniform smothered with mud and dust.

"Nothing like a trained dog for this job," said the A.R.P. man.

"He's not trained," snapped Vasatko. "He's just a bloody good dog."

They started to dig where Antis had paused. Within a quarter of an hour they had a woman out. Three of the armorers carried her to the waiting ambulance. She was still unconscious.

Midnight found them working. Most of the personnel

of the camp had joined them. There had been no return of the raiders. The civilian working parties had gathered in force. At one time Jan counted at least five such groups, digging and hauling. The street filled with ambulances. The beams of the torchlights flashed and danced over the ruins. At intervals the injured would be unearthed, lifted from the debris, and carried away. There seemed no end to this terrible night, but there had been no outbreak of fire. At two in the morning the Squadron Leader passed the word round that airmen should return to camp. They began to leave in twos and threes, disheveled and bedraggled.

Jan stood by Stetka in the roofless ruins of a house where Antis had led them. His coat was matted, his paws cut and bleeding.

"We'll get Antis to station sick quarters when we get back and have him attended to," said Stetka.

A strip of wallpaper hanging loose from the wall started to flap like a flag. There were still embers in the remains of a grate beneath a broken mantelpiece. A clock ticked defiantly in an undamaged glass cover. Above the broken mantelpiece a partition to the next room reached only shoulder high.

"There's nothing here," said Stetka. "Let's get going."

But Antis was whining again, straining at the leash, and dragging Jan after him towards the adjoining room.

"No more, boy," said Jan. "We've had enough. We've——"

The crash of the falling wall cut the rest of the sentence short. He had scarcely time to spring back, colliding with Stetka, before the partition collapsed. Stetka, choking and spluttering again, switched on the torch.

"Well, I'll be damned," said Stetka. "Are you all right?"

"I'm all right," said Jan. "We're fools to wait here."

"Where's the dog?" said Stetka.

He flashed the torch towards the mantelpiece and the grate. There was nothing but a heap of rubbish as high as their heads. The severed lead hung limply from Jan's hand.

"I don't know," said Jan, in a dull, flat voice. "I don't know."

"I'll get help," said Stetka.

He stepped over the crumbling wall and called down the street. Running footsteps sounded, and two airmen came in by the garden gate.

Jan was afraid he knew quite well where Antis was—under the pile of bricks and rubble. The broken lead in his hand had been severed as neatly as by the stroke of a knife.

The shattered room seemed full of people and light. He could recognize the hurt, indignant voice of the A.R.P. worker of the early evening.

"Not the dog! Damn it! *Not* the dog!"

Then he himself was on his knees, digging with his bare hands, flinging splintered wood and chunks of plaster in every direction on either side.

"Take it easy, now. Take it easy, Jan."

Stetka was beside him swinging a pick.

Take it easy! What the hell was Stetka talking about? These bloody Germans had killed his dog. He shouted in a voice fit to raise the dead:

"Antis! Antis!"

The answer came at once. From behind the rubble a dog barked, again and again. It was no bark of a mortally wounded animal, it was loud and clear. And it came from the now isolated room next door.

They broke their way through within minutes. The little bedroom was like a cell, knee-deep in debris. A woman was sprawled on her back under the mass of plaster as dead as anything they had ever seen. But in the far corner Antis stood by a cot. He was still barking when they led him away, and the little child in the cot was still breathing and alive.

3

On October 16, 1940, Jan received a letter from Karel with heartbreaking news. Joska, operating from East Wretham, had been killed in a crash. He was the first of the seven friends to go. A month later, Karel himself was to die.

That evening, Jan, Josef, Mirek, and Stetka met in their hut, and were joined by Jicha, who was fast becoming an ace fighter-pilot. As they talked together of Joska and luck, and the two hundred operational hours that constituted their tour in Bomber Command, Antis began displaying his alarm signals.

"There's somebody about who's not friendly," said Mirek.

"Liverpool's got a warning, but the station siren hasn't gone," said Jicha.

"The dog knows," said Stetka.

The enemy came in scarcely fifty feet over the roof of the hut, dropping five-second delayed-action bombs and zooming back to the sky before the station defenses could reply.

Jan was blown off his feet by the blast. The airmen, rushing toward the door to get to the shelter, found it jammed.

"Out of the way," roared Stetka.

At the impact of his massive body, the door disappeared into the night with Stetka somersaulting after it. Searchlights reeled across the sky. The air shuddered with gunfire and shells and the roar of engines. As Jan scrambled out into the open, he could see a second raider careering directly toward him.

"Shelter," Jan shouted to Antis. "Shelter!"

The dog sped like an arrow in the direction of the dugout. For one moment Jan saw him silhouetted against the glare almost on the threshold of the shelter, then, with devastating concussion, the first bomb of the second "stick" exploded. For the second time, the blast caught Jan. He struck the ground with such force that he lost consciousness.

He opened his eyes to find Stetka bending over him. His own mouth was full of dirt and his ears felt as if red-hot skewers were puncturing the drums. The crash of explosions was reverberating all around him. He tried to turn his head but an excruciating pain at the base of his skull made him cry out.

"Are you all right?" cried Stetka. "My God, that was a narrow squeak!"

"I'm all right," said Jan, and passed his hand over his mouth. Blood was dribbling from his nostrils and his chin was cut.

"Where's Antis?" he said.

In his mind, like a photographic negative, was the statuelike form of the dog poised on the threshold of the dugout, head turned in his direction, in the vivid glare of shimmering light.

"He's all right," said Stetka. "The last I saw of him he was making for shelter as if the wrath of God was on his tail."

Jan rose painfully to his feet. Behind him in the billowing smoke he could see where their huts had stood, a little bit of splintered matchboard.

"Mirek and Jicha are all right," said Stetka. "God, we were lucky."

"I must find Antis," said Jan.

He made his way to the dugout. Half a dozen airmen in steel helmets were emerging as he reached the concrete steps.

"Have you seen my dog?"

Nobody had seen Antis. After the bomb had dropped everything had been confused. He certainly wasn't in the shelter now, they said.

Jan went down to look but there was no sign of Antis.

He ran back to the other shelter by the N.A.A.F.I. Antis was friendly with the girls that worked there. But he was not there.

He joined Stetka and Mirek standing disconsolate by the ruins of their former quarters. On the way he avoided the gaping pit of a crater with the fresh earth scattered round its edge.

The three now searched all night. They looked in every dugout and slit trench, in every hut which remained standing, into every container, and behind the bushes on the perimeter. There was not a sign of Antis.

As dawn broke they returned to the stricken area round the N.A.A.F.I. It had occurred to Jan, now approaching the depths of despair, that the dog perhaps wounded and dying, had attempted to return to his former home.

A white rope now encircled the blackened space. A delayed-action bomb had been discovered beneath the remains of a hut and the area was out of bounds to all airmen until the demolition party had done their work.

The Armament Officer in charge, on Jan's urgent pleading to take a chance and continue his search within the restricted area, told him in no uncertain terms to get to hell out of it.

Stetka and Mirek slept in the new quarters found for them near the Lockheed hangars, but Jan toured the surrounding countryside till the following morning. At ten o'clock, unshaven and unwashed, he returned to the site by the N.A.A.F.I. But the white rope was still in position. Somewhere in the wreckage Antis could be dying.

At dawn of the following day Jan was once more back at the same site. His seat at his mahogany bomber had been empty for over twenty-four hours. Nor had he eaten. At midday the white rope was removed. Airmen of all sections, aware of the catastrophe to the dog, formed search parties during the day in their off-duty hours. Led by Jan, whistling and calling, they scoured the area. Nobody interfered. There was no sign of Antis, nor could Jan rest.

Mirek, in desperation, carried food to his friend. Grimed and unshaven, Jan refused it.

"I just can't eat," he said.

At dawn of the third day three armorers passed a stray dog moving across the blackened patch by the N.A.A.F.I. At first they took little notice of the stranger who seemed smaller and darker than the dog they had known. Then they saw that he was lame and his coat was matted with blood and mud. They picked him up, because he was weak with exhaustion through exposure and incessant efforts to force his way out of a living tomb to rejoin a beloved master, who had apparently deserted him in his hour of bitter need. They carried him, feebly wagging his tail in answer to the name of Antis, to the sergeants' mess and asked for Jan Bozdech.

Then, they hurriedly left. The last they saw, the haggard, wild-eyed man, whom they would scarcely have known, was on his knees with his arms clasped around the muddy, bloodstained dog, whom they had nearly failed to recognize.

1

On November 22, Jan, Josef, and Stetka were transferred to No. 311 (Czech) Squadron of Bomber Command, R.A.F. Station, Honington. The camp, where crews were trained in the Wellingtons they were to fly, had all the comforts of a prewar camp. The sergeants' mess was separate, and all N.C.O.'s shared a room with just one other.

Antis was by now fully recovered. They all arrived on a wet Wednesday morning, and by midday were installed in comfortable quarters amid many old friends. On Thursday, Jan decided to see the Station Warrant Officer and make the usual application to keep a dog in the camp. A clause in the Mess Rules posted on the notice board read that no animals were permitted in N.C.O.'s rooms. It had so far escaped Jan's attention. He had made his dog's bed up as usual on a blanket beside his own bed.

The Station Warrant Officer in those days could command a great deal of power. He flew no airplane and had no "trade" except for discipline. His position as a nontechnician among experts was always difficult. Sometimes, like the little girl with a curl in the middle of her forehead, he could be very nice, and at other times he could be the other thing.

Mr. Meade, of nineteen years' service, could be as formidable as he looked. He was tall, elegant, and straight as a ramrod. The thread of moustache on his upper lip might have been plucked. His eyes were a slaty, penetrating grey. He knew his business with all the thoroughness and prejudice of the regular airman.

Mr. Meade looked right through Jan, smiled his wintry smile, and handed the application to his orderly for onward transmission. The next day, Jan called at the Orderly Room and found that his application had been granted. Delighted, he returned to his room to tell Josef.

Josef indicated a note lying on Jan's bed. A feeling of foreboding went through Jan as he turned it over in his hand. Then he opened it. Sergeant Bozdech's attention was drawn to Mess Rule No. 18, which forbade any animal in the sleeping quarters of the sergeants' mess. Sergeant Bozdech was given two hours to remove the dog from his room. It was signed by Mr. Meade.

It was useless for Jan to be indignant. He and his companions were exiles and serving members of England's armed forces. They had taken an oath of allegiance and this was the least of the rules to which they must conform. Even Stetka felt that the position was hopeless.

"Very well," said Jan. "We'll find somewhere else."

He left the building, walking over the grounds in a blind fury, Antis trotting beside him. It was bitterly cold. He walked, thinking of a thousand schemes of revenge, over the airfield, to the perimeter boundary. Honington was the last place on earth, he thought, until just beyond the boundary he saw the six derelict huts. He approached the first hut and looked through the cracked window.

There was a rusty stove in the center, with a crooked chimney reaching to the roof, and a pile of old newspapers in a corner.

He tried the door and found it open. But no light appeared when he pressed the switch.

"This is our new home," he said to Antis.

Then he went back to the sergeants' mess and collected his blankets. Stetka and Josef helped him carry them but they seemed to think that he was wandering in his mind.

They helped Jan collect firewood and tried to start a fire in the stove. At the third attempt the damp newspaper began to smoulder. Josef went outside and looked up at the roof.

"There's not much of a fire in here," he said on his return, "but a hell of a lot of smoke's outside. When somebody spots it there's going to be just one hell of a row."

"They can spot what they like," said Jan.

"You'll probably get murdered in your sleep," said Stetka.

"I couldn't care less," said Jan.

By the end of the third week he was becoming accustomed to sleeping on the floor. He dared not start a fire during the day, and it was very cold at night. But he was not unhappy. The dog was provided for, the Station Warrant Officer had receded into the background, and he himself was flying again. In the evenings he used his mess, where he took his meals and drank with his friends. He even attended local dances. It was rapidly becoming a much better war and very soon he would be flying against the enemy. Only his bed, with three blankets and a greatcoat, was cold. Antis had the fourth blanket.

Often at night, in the lonely hut, separated from all the other company by the width of the windy airfield, with the fire in the worn-out stove spluttering to its last gasp, he would talk in the light of a guttering candle to his only companion. Side by side they would sit huddled together for warmth, the man with his arm around the dog and as the one talked till his eyes began to twitch with sleep, the other as if in answer would growl, deep and low in his throat, till both turned to their blankets and slept.

At midnight a fortnight before Christmas, Mr. Meade and his Orderly Corporal spent a brief forty minutes attempting to accost and challenge the hangar guard, who had somehow evaded them up to this moment.

"All right, then," he said to his colleague, "we'll catch up with the clot on the way back. Meanwhile we'll have a look round. There's a gale warning."

The Orderly Corporal cursed under his breath and smilingly complied. They strode across the darkened airfield together. When they had finished inspection and were about to retrace their steps, a sudden stirring of the breeze carried a whiff of pungent smoke in their direction.

"Where's that smoke coming from?" asked the Orderly Officer.

"I don't notice nothing," said the Orderly Corporal, who wanted to get to bed.

"You're not alert," said Mr. Meade. "If that is not smoke, then I'm a Hottentot!"

The Orderly Corporal mumbled an apology, and agreed that there was a "peculiar pong" now he came to think of it.

"It's coming from the old transit huts that visiting crews used in the old days," said the Station Warrant Officer. "Poachers or some such. We'll cut over."

It was no poacher they discovered, but Antis and his master, rolled in blankets before a stove just made up for the night with green fuel.

Mr. Meade flashed his torch past the door he'd flung open and said in a very loud voice:

"What are you doing here, may I ask?"

Jan sat up, rubbing the sleep out of his eyes. The beam of the torch full in his face was disconcerting.

"Who the devil are you?" said Mr. Meade, and then in answer to his own question: "If it isn't one of those Czech foreigners. It's Sergeant Bozdech and his bleeding bloodhound."

Antis, sensitive to the antagonistic tone, was on his feet, hackles raised. He began to growl, so that the Orderly Corporal made the clucking noise of appeasement.

"Who gave you permission to take up your quarters here?" said the S.W.O.

"You turned me out of my room," said Jan, "so we had to find somewhere."

"Nobody turned you out of the mess," said Mr. Meade. "You were merely asked to comply with a standing Mess Rule."

"Where my dog goes, I go," said Jan.

"Is that so?" said Mr. Meade slowly and deliberately. "Now, is that so?"

The Orderly Corporal had taken his notebook and pencil out and his eye was on his superior.

"Take his name," said the S.W.O. "To report to my office after parade tomorrow morning. We'll see about this."

He turned on his heel and left the hut.

Jan lay sleepless on the hard bed. The cold crept into his bones and soul. It seemed to him that since he had looked over the broken door in a shattered farmhouse near the Siegfried Line and stared down into a puppy's shining eyes the ties that bound them together had grown and strengthened to the unyielding grip of iron. What was the end to be? Very shortly now, he would be taking a gunner's seat behind the twin Brownings in the face of the enemy. Nor might he return.

But he knew what he'd do the following morning. Even before they went on parade he would go to an old friend, Flight Lieutenant Davis, and, if need be, haul him out of bed to plead his cause.

He had no need to drag the Flight Lieutenant from his bed at eight o'clock the next day for he found him shaving. Jan apologized in a torrent of incoherence.

The Flight Lieutenant, a man of good sense and understanding, said, dabbing his chin with a towel, "All right! All right! Don't take it so much to heart, Jan. I'll see the Station Adjutant and maybe the C.O. at breakfast. If their livers are functioning after last night's Guest Night, I've no doubt something can be done."

Jan went on morning parade and then, shaking with trepidation, made his call on the Station Warrant Officer.

But words had passed, those mysterious words that come from an august person to one less august, and often take immediate effect.

"Ah! Yes," said Mr. Meade. "Ah! Yes, Sergeant Bozdech. I've seen the Commanding Officer and it has been decided to take no further action in this matter. Report for your duties as usual."

"Thank you, sir," said Jan.

"Not at all," said Mr. Meade, still hearing the echo of

that more august voice, saying: "For pity's sake, Mr. Meade, do bear in mind that these poor bastards have come the hell of a way to fight on our side and it is up to us to show a spot of tact."

"It might be possible," Mr. Meade went on, "to rescind that particular clause about animals in sergeants' bunks————"

"Please not to bother, sir," said Jan. "You've been to enough trouble on my behalf. I do thank you very much. Antis and I are really quite happy where we are——"

"Just as you wish," said Mr. Meade. "And now, if you don't mind————"

He picked up a file.

"Good morning, sir, and thank you," said Jan.

"Good morning," said the S.W.O., sighing deeply as the door closed on a jubilant sergeant.

That evening when Jan entered the hut he found a fire roaring in the stove, and a supply of dry firewood and coal. Moreover, there were two extra blankets, and under the window a new writing desk.

He thought of Mr. Meade almost with affection, but when his eye fell on a Wellington aircraft, black against the rose and daffodil sky of a fine November dusk, then those other darker thoughts returned. He called his dog to his side and patted his head.

Across the airdrome, the red of the sky was reflected in one unwinking window of the Watch Office. Very soon the duty pilot would be changing watch. Red sky at night, it was going to be a fine day tomorrow! He cuffed the dog lightly.

"Come along, you villain," he said. "Let's go and buy some beer."

2

Christmas had come and gone. It had been a tremendous occasion. Now on New Year's Day, Stetka, Josef, and Jan, having completed their course, were flying to their post at No. 311 Squadron, East Wretham.

It was a fine, crisp day. From the air the snow-flat countryside scintillated in the early sunlight. As they prepared to land Jan could see the bomb-trailers towed by their tractors across the airfield beneath. The familiar sight startled him in its significance. Very soon now, he too would be one of a crew speeding into the night, bound for a distant target.

Then they were coming in to land and he could see Vlasta waiting with Ludva and Gustav. They clapped him on the back and wrung him by the hand the moment he alighted. Antis, wild with excitement at the sight of his old friends, pranced and leaped and ran in circles so that Vlasta cried:

"Look at the dog! Look at the dog! He's doing a war dance for joy."

The phrase was to stick for many a day. They took Jan and the rest of the crew to their quarters in the newly requisitioned Manor Farm. Jan and his dog were to share an upper room with Ludva, while Gustav and Josef were next door. The bare boards and scanty furniture were in great contrast to Honington, but the friends were reunited.

The farm lay north of the airfield; to the right, on the main road, lay Squadron headquarters and the sergeants' mess. The village of East Wretham itself straggled down the road to the east.

Flying was desultory. In the last three weeks of January the weather closed in with fog. Jan, as forward gunner in "C" for Cecilia, found his place with his crew and settled down into Squadron life.

It was far from unpleasant, despite the damp and the bitter cold. The farmyard of the Manor Farm soon filled with ancient cars, motorcycles, and push bikes, anything which could get to the bars of "The Ark Royal" or "The Bell." Often of an evening Group Captain Pickard, and Wing Commander Josef Ocelka would visit the saloons and mix with the boys. Pickard liked the Czechs; they in turn thought the world of this gallant and able man.

Jan acquired a secondhand bicycle and rode daily to the airdrome with Antis trotting beside him. Frequently they would hunt together in the neighboring woods. It was an excellent life for a dog learning his way around.

He could now be trusted to look after himself on the airfield. He would never approach an aircraft in motion or with its engine running. Jan, fearful of an accident, had previously, at Honington, arranged with the assistance of the ground crew to catch the dog with the blast of the slip stream. Antis never again ventured near any aircraft with engines running.

Now at East Wretham, with the aid of his bicycle, Jan completed the training of preventing the dog from crossing the airfield, thereby confining himself to the use of the perimeter track only.

Patiently, Jan used a simple method: At the first attempt that Antis made to take an obvious short cut across the grass, Jan would shout "No" in a loud and determined voice. Often, Jan would dismount from his bicycle, and embracing the landing ground with a comprehensive sweep of his hand and a forefinger under the dog's nose, would say, stressing each word: "Never again." In this fashion, with repeating the lesson two or three times over a period of a fortnight, and never infringing his own golden rule by crossing over the grass, Jan succeeded in driving the lesson home. Moreover, it was not long before Antis could understand the meaning of simple words such as "wait," "come," "sit," "lie down," "no," and "fetch." Much training had gone before, but during the inclement weather, the opportunity arose to exercise the dog's intelligence. It was a labor of love and patience.

In the years to come the association between the two was to reach the point where it was only necessary for Jan to mutter aloud: "I wonder who's going to shut the door," when Antis, settled down on his rug, would rise and force the door to with his head and complete its closing with a final thrust of a paw.

As the weather cleared in February and flying recommenced, a further manifestation of the dog's remarkable sense in detecting the approach of aircraft became apparent.

By the second week of February, Jan was flying regularly against the enemy at night. The ground crew of four mechanics responsible for servicing Cecilia under the direction of Corporal Adam, or "Adamek," had grown to know Antis very well.

It was to Adamek that Jan trusted his dog and from whom he learned what occurred in his absence.

Antis would watch Jan as he climbed into his airplane. As "C" for Cecilia took her place in the queue on the runway, the dog would begin to tremble with excitement. So he would remain till the last aircraft vanished into the sky, standing thereafter for long minutes gazing after the Squadron. Then, his tail between his legs, he would take up his resting place by the side of the mechanics' tent. Neither Adamek nor his companions could induce him to move. When they departed for supper the dog would go to sleep.

Some hours later, according to the length of the trip, probably on the approach of dawn, Antis would awake. He would lie very still, his eyes open, his ears moving. Those on standby would know that the Squadron was returning.

But it was only when Antis sprang to his feet and began to whine that they knew "C" for Cecilia was on its way. He had taught himself to detect the particular pitch of the airscrews of the machine that carried his master. Then he would begin the boundings and prancing around the mechanics that had become known as his "war dance."

By the middle of March, Jan had completed ten trips.

Gustav and his crew had failed to return from a raid on Bremen. Shot down but surviving, they became prisoners of war.

At the same time Group Captain Pickard was selected as the pilot of "F" for Freddie in the first of the wartime documentary films *Target for Tonight*. Wing Commander Ocelka took over the actual handling of the Squadron.

In the last week of March, King George VI and the Queen visited East Wretham. It was snowing and the air-raid warning sounded as the Royal Party was due to arrive. No enemy attack developed, but Antis, sitting in front of his own crew, offered a paw to the Queen as she passed before him. They exchanged salutations.

Three days later Stetka and his crew were shot down in flames over Dusseldorf.

Jan had now completed half his tour. Antis had begun to take an interest in the night life of the neighboring woods, but he was invariably back by dawn to greet "C" for Cecilia.

Most of the villagers had grown to know and respect Antis. It was an Air Ministry Warden who understood neither countryside nor airplanes who was to promote trouble for Antis.

3

The warden stood at the gap in the hedge which led to the airfield, his little hut behind him. His duty was restricted to controlling traffic on its way to camp. He was officially ranked as a Service policeman.

Five nights after Stetka had been killed, "C" for Cecilia was one of a sortie, detailed for night attack on Osnabruck. The crews climbed into their lorry, bound for the crew room to pick up their parachutes. The lorry was overcrowded and Jan decided to send Antis on ahead. He knew his way and could be trusted to keep off the airfield. There was plenty of time.

Antis set off as he had done many times before. Wing Commander Ocelka was away on official business and the Squadron Adjutant, Flight Lieutenant Snaider, had gotten sick. His place had been temporarily filled by the Station Adjutant, whose main interest was in maintaining discipline, particularly in regard to flying personnel, whom he regarded as spoiled and pampered.

As Antis drew level with the entrance to the airfield the warden shouted "sheer off," at him. The dog halted for a moment, and then, satisfied the order could not be for him, continued on his way. No one else was about, except four fitters belonging to "B" Flight, who knew Antis and his reputation.

The warden shouted again and thrust his bicycle across the dog's path.

This was not according to the rules and Jan was nowhere in sight. The dog, faced by this obstinate man and his contraption of wire and steel, decided to jump the hedge to the perimeter track. As he was about to leap the bicycle swung again and the pedal struck his nose.

The blow hurt. The dog's hackles rose as he started to growl. The warden, alarmed, backed away, the bicycle outthrust before him. The four fitters called to the dog. He made the merest sign of recognition and then continued his advance on his enemy. His growl grew louder. The warden, now thoroughly alarmed, retreated backwards towards his hut. But he was two yards wrong, and went into a deep, muddy ditch, his bicycle on top of him.

Antis turned and ran through the gap in the hedge. The four fitters, struggling to control their laughter, climbed into the ditch to help the man out. He was plastered with mud and wet through. But Antis was racing round the perimeter to keep his appointment.

That night, "C" for Cecilia returned home well before dawn. Antis and his master slept the sound sleep of those with untroubled consciences.

The following morning the Orderly Sergeant woke Jan with a rough shake of his shoulder.

"You're to report to the Adjutant's office."

"Is he back?" said Jan. "What's the time?"

"No, he's not back; he's still sick," said the Orderly Sergeant. "It's the Station Adjutant at S.H.Q."

"Oh, that old martinet," said Jan. "What's he belly-aching about?"

"I wouldn't know," said the Orderly Sergeant. "It's five past ten. You'd better get a move on."

"I'm stood down," said Jan. "I was operating last night."

Nevertheless, he climbed out of bed, shaved, and dressed. It was unfair; all crews were allowed to lie in after a trip and if it had been their own Adjutant it wouldn't have happened. He wondered what on earth he could be wanted for. Nevertheless, it was a fine morning and they'd survived another trip. He was whistling to himself as he reached S.H.Q. with Antis. They passed the Air Ministry warden on the way.

"Good morning," said Jan. The man made no reply, but the grin on his face was smug. Antis passed him with his head in the air.

The Adjutant was sitting bolt upright in his chair, his arms folded. He looked, Jan thought, like the wrath of God.

"You sent for me, sir?" said Jan.

"That dog's got to go," said the Adjutant.

"Dog, sir?" said Jan bewildered. "My dog, got to go?"

"He must be removed from the camp at once."

"But he's the Squadron mascot, sir. Everybody knows that."

"You've no official permit to keep a dog on the camp."

"Group Captain Pickard never wanted one, sir. He knew all about this dog. He liked him."

"The Group Captain isn't the Station Commander any longer. You were never issued a permit, and I have before me a report from an Air Ministry warden that your dog savagely attacked him last night. We're guests in this country and we've got to conform."

"It's the first I've heard of any attack, sir," said Jan.

"Do you think the British police make a serious charge like this without foundation? The dog drove the warden off his bicycle and into the ditch. It's all here, chapter and verse."

"It's a lie, sir!" said Jan.

"You can retract that remark at once, else I shall have to deal with *you* as well."

"But it doesn't make sense, sir! Antis isn't savage."

"The Station Warrant Officer has a letter for you telling you what I have decided. Sign it when you've read it. Then carry out my instructions."

The letter was brief. Forty-eight hours were granted to find a home for Antis, otherwise the dog would be destroyed.

Jan returned to the Adjutant's office.

"I should like to see the Commanding Officer, please, sir."

"The Wing Commander's not here. He's away at Air Ministry."

"The C.O. would never agree to your decision, sir."

"In the Wing Commander's absence my instruction stands."

"You know I can't find a home for Antis in forty-eight hours," said Jan, exasperated. "This is a put-up job. Do you know the history behind this dog?"

"I don't want to have to send you for court martial," said the Adjutant. "Don't drive me too far."

"You can do what you bloody well like," said Jan, "but you're not going to take my dog from me when there's no just cause."

He tore the letter into fragments and dropped them into the wastepaper basket. The Adjutant regarded him with steely calm.

"I should put you under close arrest," he said, "but you are operating tonight. When the Wing Commander returns I shall see that he deals with you. As regards your dog, you know my instructions. Get out of here before I lose my temper."

Jan went back to the sergeants' mess, trembling with rage and indignation. He was certain that Antis, unprovoked, would never have attacked anybody. Something had gone very wrong, but what it might be there was no means of discovering, and the uncorroborated word of the warden could send the dog to his death.

Everyone in the mess agreed that this would never have happened if the "old man" had been there.

Something had to be done. Antis was the Squadron mascot. Cynics could dismiss that sort of superstition as nonsense, but it fortified morale; and the dog was a symbol from their earliest days together. Their lives were bound up with his. It was unthinkable that an outsider could destroy what they had cherished for so long.

That afternoon, after "C" for Cecilia had been checked over for the next operation, Jan had the germ of an idea. With Antis, he went to see Old Colly who lived in his cottage at the far end of the wood.

The old villager and Jan had been friends ever since Jan's first evening at East Wretham. Old Colly had admired Antis from the beginning and knew his story. Moreover, the occupation of his village by the Czechs had caught his fancy. He was a simple and amiable soul, with a reputation as a poacher in his younger days. His stories enthralled Jan, and many a time he had sought out the old fellow, bringing him an ounce of tobacco or a pound of tea for his wife. Now he was bent on finding Old Colly and enlisting his services.

He found the old man digging in his garden. Jan came to the point at once.

"Do away with your dog!" cried Old Colly, as Jan concluded. "Damn impertinence, I call it! I'll settle their hash."

Jan couldn't have had a more ready accomplice. The flouting of any kind of authority was the spice of life to the old rascal, whose villainies had never exceeded the disappearance of a sitting pheasant or the illegitimate maintenance of a couple of ferrets.

"Come with me," said Old Colly. "We'll learn 'em."

He led the way to the back of his garden where under a tangle of weed and bramble lay a trap door to a cellar.

"Runs under the cottage," said Old Colly. "The missus and me used it for to store 'taters in days gone by. If it were dry enough for 'taters, 'tis fit enough for a dog."

They cleared the weed and drew the bolt. The cellar yawned dark beneath them but there was even a glimmer of light from a ventilator at one end.

"We'll clean it out," said Old Colly, "in no time at all. They'll never think of looking here, they're that ignorant."

They cleaned out the cellar between them. The old man had been quite right; it was dry and airy. Then, leaving Antis with him, Jan returned to his billet, collected some of his clothes, and carried them back. Their presence would reassure the dog.

"He should be safe here with me," said Old Colly. "I'll see to his food and water and let him out for a minute or two at night for his own affairs when there's nary a soul about."

He rubbed his hands together till the knuckle joints cracked.

"My word!" he said. "What a proper caper it is, to be sure, and me at my age." He was delighted with himself.

Two days passed. Twice, with two friends posted to watch, Jan took Antis out for exercise. The dog had given no trouble to the cottager and his wife. On the third night, with the Squadron stood down, Jan moved into the cellar himself. The forty-eight hours' grace was at an end, but by Monday the Wing Commander should be back.

On the Saturday afternoon Jan was sitting on the wall of the farmyard with his friend Serg. Leo Andrele, whom he had known in Czechoslovakia. Andrele had promised to spend the following night in the cellar, when Jan would again be operating. There was hardly a soul on the station who wouldn't have done his best to see an end to this sorry business. It was becoming the talk of the camp, but not an airman would have betrayed Jan.

"Hello," said Andrele, "look who's visiting us."

"I knew they were coming," said Jan. "The S.W.O. tipped me off." Andrele grinned. Everybody was in it.

The Station Adjutant with the Orderly Sergeant and his corporal came in by the farmyard gate. Jan and Andrele stood to attention, and saluted as the party passed.

"Would you believe it!" said Sergeant Andrele. They could hear the progress of the search as boots clattered on bare boards and doors slammed. The Adjutant returned to the farmyard, crimson in the face and perspiring. For the moment they paused in the porch Jan thought he was to be summoned, but the Adjutant turned on his heel and made off round the back of the premises. As the corporal passed Jan on his way out he was beaming all over his face.

The corporal returned ten minutes later. Jan was again perched on the wall with Andrele.

"Sergeant Bozdech to report to the Station Adjutant's office immediately," said the corporal.

He glanced around him to make sure they were alone.

"They've come forward," he whispered in confidential tones, "all four of them."

"Who's come forward?" asked Andrele.

"Four fitters from 'B' Flight," said the corporal. "The ones that saw what happened last Monday night. They helped pull the policeman out of the ditch."

"What did they say?" said Jan eagerly.

"That it wasn't the dog's fault. He was provoked."

"My God!" said Andrele. "You're cleared, Jan."

"That," said Jan, knowing his enemy, "remains to be seen."

He went across to Station Headquarters and into the Adjutant's office. That officer's face was purple.

"Where's that dog of yours?" he demanded.

"I'm sorry, sir, but I couldn't carry out your orders."

"I shall have you court-martialled."

"If you feel that's what you must do, sir, then that's what you'll have to do."

"Very well, then."

Jan made a last plea.

"I couldn't carry out an order that I know Wing Commander Ocelka would never approve of. I don't want to flout your authority, sir, but there are four airmen who saw what took place that night. I do beg of you, sir————"

"I am not interested in your witnesses. You're all together in this. They'd swear anything to save the dog because he's popular. If you imagine for one moment that I am prepared to lose the co-operation of the British Police for a dog, you're mistaken. Now get out of my office!"

That night, a civilian police search was conducted for a "savage Alsatian" as requested by the Station Adjutant. The search in Colly's cottage occurred simultaneously with the take-off of "C" for Cecilia.

Sergeant Andrele had to kick out the candle and clap his hand across Antis's muzzle at the same time, for the dog began to bark when he heard the plane's engines. It was an hour before the sergeant took his hand from the dog's collar and looked outside. All was quiet. Nobody came down the road that night.

At noon on Monday, a clerk who risked facing a charge for his absence, brought Jan the news that Wing Commander Ocelka had returned. Jan immediately went to the Station Adjutant's office and boldly requested an interview with his Commanding Officer.

"Quite impossible," said the Station Adjutant. "He's far too busy."

"The matter is urgent, sir," insisted Jan.

Out of the corner of his eye he could see that the door leading to the Wing Commander's office was ajar.

"The C.O. is only just back. He can't see anybody."

A well-known voice called through the open door.

"Is that you, Jan?"

"Yes, sir," said Jan, with beating heart.

"Come on in."

Wing Commander Ocelka was sitting on the corner of

his desk reading a file. He threw it into his tray as Jan entered.

"How have you been coping?" he said.

"We've done three trips in your absence," said Jan. "But I'm in trouble. Bad trouble, sir."

The Wing Commander's face clouded.

"Not in the air," Jan assured him hastily. "On the ground, sir."

"That's different," said Ocelka grinning. "That's nothing new for you. What's it this time? Have you got her telephone number? How's Antis?"

"It's about Antis I want to see you, sir."

There was a knock at the door and the Adjutant came in.

"When you were in London, sir," he said, "this sergeant's dog attacked a policeman and I had to take immediate action."

"It's the first I've heard of it," said Ocelka. "Why didn't you tell me on the 'phone? I rang you up each day."

"It seemed a straightforward enough case, sir. I didn't want to trouble you unnecessarily."

"Nothing's any trouble that concerns the personnel of my Squadron. What's Antis been up to, Jan? I've never known him vicious."

The Adjutant withdrew. At the conclusion of Jan's story, the Wing Commander rang for a copy of the Adjutant's letter of instructions. Then, calling a clerk, he dictated a permit for the dog in English and Czech. It concluded:

"The dog is of a friendly nature and it is considered unnecessary to keep him on a lead."

"And that," said the Wing Commander, "solves that."

"Thank you, sir," said Jan.

"Sometime in the future," said Ocelka, "you may run across a Station Commander who hasn't any time for animals. If you ever get into trouble again with Antis let me know. I'll do my best for you if I'm still in circulation, and if anything happens to you I'll look after the dog. I'll give you sixty pounds now for him if you like."

"I wouldn't part with him. Not even to you, sir."

"I thought you'd say that. But they're hostages to fortune, Jan. Sometimes I think none of us should add to our responsibilities at a time like this."

"I've thought of that, sir," said Jan, thinking now of his Wing Commander's young wife, still in Czechoslovakia, who was attempting to escape and rejoin her husband.

"Well, we'll have to leave it at that, I suppose," said Ocelka.

"Very good, sir," said Jan, and left.

I

On June 22, 1941, Hitler invaded Russia, and on the same date No. 311 Squadron was detailed for night attack on the marshaling yards at Hamm. It was one of the shorter trips, being four and a half hours. "C" for Cecilia was one of the detail.

When the last of the sortie had disappeared into the summer night Antis accompanied Corporal Adamek and his mechanics into their hut. The ground crew would remain till the Squadron returned without troubling to go back to their mess. Other ground crew would join them. Adamek possessed a pack of cards.

Seven men sat down to play whist. The dog lay at the corporal's feet. From time to time he would pad across to the flap of the tent and nose it open. Nowadays when Jan was on a mission Antis would often creep away to the adjacent woods and hunt in silent delight. He was seldom successful, but his pleasure was intense. It was as if he had grown to accept his master's absence and had granted himself a few hours' respite.

"What's the matter with the dog?" said Kubicek. "He seems very restive. Are we expecting visitors?"

It was past midnight.

"No," said Adamek. "Those are not his usual reactions." He called Antis to him.

"Go and find your playmates in the wood," he said. *"Rabbits."* The dog pricked up his ears and his tail twitched.

"Rabbits," Adamek repeated.

Antis shot him a glance and turned away. He moved to the corporal's side and laid a paw on his knee.

"What's the matter?" said Adamek. He put down his cards and took the dog's head between his hands.

"What's troubling you?" he said.

Antis went to the door again and pushed the flap aside. He stood sniffing the night air.

"Damn the dog," said another mechanic. "Why can't he make up his mind?"

Adamek crossed over and leant down beside Antis. He put his arm round him.

"It's too early," he said. "He won't be back yet. Go off to the woods."

The dog thrust his muzzle under the man's arm. Adamek could feel him quivering with excitement.

"Oh, come on!" said the mechanic. "It's your deal."

"Shut up," said Adamek. "There's something up."

He removed the dog's head from beneath his arm and began to rub the base of Antis's ears.

"They'll be on their way back," he said, "but they won't be here yet. Oh! Why the hell can't these animals talk? What are you trying to say, boy? What's the matter with you?"

The dog was beginning to whine and shiver. Suddenly he lifted his head. The sound of that one long, drawn, piercing howl could be heard in the stillness of the night right across the airdrome.

The battered alarm clock in the tent pointed to one o'clock in the morning.

2

The clock in the pilot's instrument panel of "C" for Cecilia pointed to a minute to one. They were over the defense zone on the Dutch coast on their way back from Hamm, caught in the searchlights and coned. Two thousand feet beneath him Jan could see two other Wellingtons caught in the white beams that swept the sky. As he watched the shellfire bursting round them and the sausagelike strings of tracers that floated past, both airplanes began to glow red. He saw the first of them disintegrate into blazing fragments.

They themselves were flying straight and level. Jan knew that Jo Capka would be taking violent evasive action if it were possible. It meant that they must have been hit. Something screeched and clattered by the side of his head. And something else biting hot struck his forehead. The sudden gust of air in his face through the shattered perspex struck him violently as the blood poured down and into his eyes. As the bank of cloud suddenly enveloped "C" for Cecilia and the glare of the searchlights in the cockpit faded the clock on the instrument panel pointed to one o'clock.

"C" for Cecilia, crippled and losing height, began her precarious passage back across the North Sea.

3

At half-past one "S" for Sylvia landed at East Wretham. She was followed by three other Wellingtons at regular intervals. The last to land was Wing Commander Ocelka in "M" for Marie. There was still no sign of "C" for Cecilia two hours later.

The ground mist had become dense. The returned aircraft had long since been silent, their cockpits covered. In their tent on the fringe of the wood Corporal Adamek and his four mechanics still waited. Kubicek said:

"It's no good hanging on much longer."

It was getting cold. All four of them went outside and stared into the sky. There was a hint of dawn in the east.

"We'll give it another quarter of an hour," said Adamek. He looked at Antis. The dog was sitting up on his haunches, perfectly motionless, staring into the east, his ears pricked forward. Every now and again he would raise a foreleg and lower it. He was beginning to whimper. Adamek moved to him and laid a hand on his head. The dog started at his touch, glanced swiftly up at him and looked away, intent once more on the sky.

Kubicek looked out of the tent. He had packed his tools and they were slung across his shoulder in their greasy canvas bag. On the far side of the airdrome by the Watch Office a car was starting up.

"Come on," said Kubicek. "I can do with some breakfast." He spoke lightly. This was the sort of occasion when emphasis must be laid on the commonplace.

"Very well," said Adamek. "Come along, Antis."

The dog never moved. Ocelka, bareheaded and still in his Irvine jacket and flying boots, drove up, the car lumbering across the grass.

"That's right," he said to Adamek, "get back to camp and get some food."

"Any news, sir?" said Kubicek.

"Not yet. Come on, Antis, come on, boy."

He flung open the door of the driving seat for the dog to jump in. The mechanics began to move across the airdrome.

"Give him a shove, Corporal," said Ocelka.

"Come along, boy," said Adamek, and forced Antis on to his hind legs, but he dug his forepaws in with stiffened joints. Adamek gave up the task and looked at Ocelka.

"I can't get him to move, sir."

The Wing Commander jumped out of his car and strode through the dewy grass.

"This is the moment I've always dreaded," he said.

He seized Antis by the collar and attempted to drag him to the car. The dog resisted with all his strength.

"It's no good, sir," said Adamek. "He won't move until Jan arrives. I know him."

"And so do I, dammit!" said Ocelka. "Perhaps he'll

change his mind when he gets hungry. Jump in, I'll give you a lift."

They drove back round the airdrome in silence. Ocelka drew up at the entrance to the airmen's mess.

"Will they be all right, sir?"

"They're supposed to have made a landfall off Orford Ness. Don't spread it around. I'll let you know when there's anything definite. Good night."

"Thank you very much, sir," said Corporal Adamek, and bade his Commanding Officer good night.

Immediately after breakfast, Ludva and Kubicek went across to visit Antis. At the sound of their approach and Ludva's voice Antis turned his head, but did not rise.

"He knows more than we do," said Ludva brokenly. "Oh, damn and damn and damn this bloody war!"

Antis, still motionless, began to whimper.

"Come on," said Ludva. "I can't stand this. Let's get out of here."

He began to blunder back the way he had come. The dog continued to whimper.

"Stop it," shouted Kubicek. "It's no good crying. That won't bring him back."

He went into the tent for a ground sheet and dropped it at his feet. Then he sat down. He began to fondle the scruff of Antis' neck. The dog, completely unresponsive, started to howl. Ground crews working on the neighboring aircraft heard the sound and rested their tools.

The clouds that had been rapidly gathering for the last hour brought a deluge. Kubicek laid the ground sheet over Antis and went into the tent. The dog had refused to budge. When the rain grew lighter Kubicek returned to the airmen's mess, collected a plate of roast liver, which Antis preferred above all else, and went back with Corporal Adamek. It was still raining.

Antis ignored the proffered dish, but they built a shelter over him with brushwood and two more ground sheets to keep off the rain. The dog's coat was drenched black and he was shivering, but both men doubted if it was with the cold.

Late in the afternoon the news came through that "C" for Cecilia had landed at Coltishall in the early hours of Monday morning and that her only casualty, Jan Bozdech, was in Norwich Hospital with a superficial wound in the forehead.

But nobody could pass on those glad tidings to a dog.

All through that night Antis kept vigil. It rained continuously, but the dog resented the shelter built above him and moved out again into the open. Adamek said it was to enable him to hear better. He remained with his muzzle on his paws till dawn, when at the witching hour of his master's customary return he sat upright again, with his ears cocked and his face to the sky. An hour after first light he once more began to howl.

Ludva brought a second plate of liver, which Antis still refused to touch, and though he tolerated Ludva's caresses, he growled menacingly when the sergeant attempted to drag him away. In the afternoon, the Wing Commander himself drove out in his car with the Padre.

The Padre, an understanding person and an admirable priest, by the name of Pouchly, listened patiently to Ocelka's diatribe on the evils that could arise when air crew on operations kept pets. Then he suggested a simple solution.

"You must forgive me, Wing Commander, but wouldn't it be an admirable idea to ask the medical authorities at Norwich if they would permit Jan Bozdech to come and fetch his dog and take it back to hospital with him?"

"Good God!" said Ocelka. "What the hell next! I beg your pardon."

"There's nothing very much wrong with Jan, and there's no reason why they can't have the dog at the hospital for a day or so."

"No truer word was ever spoken!" exclaimed Ocelka. "Come, Padre. We'll go and ring them up right away."

Twelve hours later Jan and his dog were together in Norwich Hospital.

4

It took no longer to repair "C" for Cecilia than it did Jan. The airman returned from hospital with a slight scar and the airplane with a permanent fault in her heating, which thereafter cut out over ten thousand feet, but within the month both were operating over enemy territory.

They crossed the Dutch coast at ten thousand feet, and the heating failed at once, but Jan, chewing raisins in the forward turret, scarcely noticed as they began to climb. He was more concerned that Antis had not been on the dispersal point to see them depart. The dog had accompanied his master to roll call. Jan had not seen him since.

It was, he supposed, a reaction that might have been expected after the long vigil of two nights in the open and the misery he had endured. He had no doubt that Antis, in service parlance, had had a bellyful. Nevertheless, he was concerned at his lapse. Then he heard the crackling of the "intercom."

"Navigator to Wireless Operator . . . can you hear me?"

He heard the appropriate reply and the Navigator's voice again.

"Am I going round the bend or do you see what I see?"

"I was going to ask you the same thing. He must have been under the bed by the flare chute."

And then Kacir again:

"Wireless Operator to Front Gunner . . . can you hear me? Over."

"I can hear you loud and clear," said Jan.

"We've a passenger."

Jan knew at once what had happened. Nobody had troubled to look at the emergency bed beneath the flare chute before take-off. He opened the partition door and ordered Antis into the turret. The dog settled down at once between his feet.

This was a pretty kettle of fish, but there was nothing to be done about it for the moment. As for Antis, he was completely at ease and appeared to be sleeping.

They went into the target at eight thousand feet. The fires beneath them were already raging. "C" for Cecilia made her run-in above the sinister balloon barrage and successfully bombed the oil refinery on the outskirts of the town.

The stream of flak burst around them, and the aircraft shuddered, but Antis, his eyes steady on his master's face, alternately lit by searchlights and the flashes of exploding shells, kept calm as long as Jan appeared unmoved. It was as if each drew strength from the other, for Jan, faced with the double responsibility of controlling himself as well as his dog, found himself more than once forcing a nod of encouragement, and as the dog took heart he renewed resolution in his master.

Halfway home an ME. 110 came in on a quarter attack. Jan gave him a burst from the twin Brownings, and the German rolled his aircraft on its back and vanished into the darkness. Jan felt with his free hand for Antis. The dog responded gratefully to his touch and moved an inch closer, resting his head on his master's knee.

In such a manner man and dog, the plane still intact, reached home safely at dawn. "M" for Marie was already in. Jan, from his turret, could see the sturdy figure of Adamek running backwards on his heels waving them in. Worried beyond measure at the absence of the dog, he was the first to greet them. At the sight of Antis capering and leaping in his "war dance" the little corporal ran up and seized Jan's arm.

"So that's where he was all the time!" said Adamek. "We've searched high and low for him."

Antis, wild with delight, sprang towards him and Adamek caught him in his arms.

"You miserable bastard," said Adamek lovingly.

"Did he behave himself?" he asked Jan.

"Perfectly," said Jan. "But I shall be for the high jump!" The dog was still running around in circles, barking joyously. As Ocelka's car drove up he galloped towards it and flung himself at the Wing Commander as he stepped out.

"You're back to your old form, I see," said Ocelka grimly. He would often, on landing, intercept a crew on their way back to Headquarters and pause for a chat on the night's activities.

"How did you make out?" he said to Capka.

The crew of "C" for Cecilia were favorites with the Wing Commander. Capka had flown with him as second pilot, and Ocelka's and Jan's paths had crossed in the early days in Poland and in the Foreign Legion.

"Fair enough, sir," said Capka. "We had a snapper on our tail for a bit on the way back, but he sheered off after a couple of bursts."

"Did you hit him, Jan?" said Ocelka.

"Not a hope, sir," said Jan.

"What about Josef?" inquired Ocelka. "I don't suppose *he* was so busily occupied." He patted Antis on the head. "What do *you* think?" he said to the dog.

"Please let me explain, sir," began Jan.

"What the eye doesn't see the heart doesn't grieve over," said Ocelka to Antis, fondling him. "Now where have I heard that before? You tell me. You're a clever dog."

He took the dog's muzzle in his hands and shook his head to and fro.

"You've a fool for a master," he said. "He talks too much. He ought to know I've enough trouble on my hands with two-legged beasts, without looking for more from those with four!"

He released the dog with a slap on the flank.

"What were you saying, Jo?" he said to the pilot as they walked off together.

Two nights later the target was Hanover. It was "C" for Cecilia's thirty-second trip, and very soon now her first tour of operations would be ending and her crew rested. There was always increased tension when the completion of a tour was approaching. More than one crew had gone in on their last trip. Each member of "C" for Cecilia's crew was feeling the strain. And now it was Hanover— one of the worst. But Antis, sublimely unaware of such anxieties, was beside himself with delight when Jan invited him into the aircraft on take-off. It was strictly against Air Ministry regulations to take an animal into the air on operations, but the dog was an accepted passenger after Ocelka's connivance.

They encountered the usual nightmare over Hanover and were fortunate to survive. But the considerable evasive action drove them off course. As they crossed the English coast, three-quarters of an hour behind time, they found the whole of East Anglia fog-bound.

It was impossible to land at East Wretham. Fog lay over the airdrome to the height of six hundred feet. The indicator needle of the fuel gauge was flickering down to zero mark.

It seemed to Jan that the end of their tour, of "C" for Cecilia, and of themselves could be close at hand. They could not land at their own base and were practically out of fuel. This, indeed, might be the luck of the draw. He looked down at the dog by his feet. Antis was sleeping peacefully.

When Capka, as captain of the aircraft, finally got in touch with Flying Control, "C" for Cecilia had already been circling the fog bank for twenty precious minutes. The advice that, at last, reached Capka was to climb to ten thousand feet, steer for the coast, and abandon the aircraft. He was also informed that the conditions over all neighboring airdromes were identical with those now beneath him. As all members of the crew of "C" for Cecilia were plugged in to the intercom, this depressing information became common property simultaneously.

None of them had ever bailed out. Jan had inveigled the station tailor to adapt an oxygen mask for Antis, but now he wondered if he should have approached the parachute section on a similar request, because he had no intention whatsoever of abandoning the dog if they had to jump. The thought of carrying an extra, living burden, struggling and frightened, was doubly alarming. He knew that he had never been so terrified in his life. Then he heard Capka on the R.T. reporting to Flying Control that he was starting to climb and make for the coast as suggested, adding that the fuel gauge had almost reached the absolute minimum reading.

In reply, to everyone's relief, Wing Commander Ocelka himself came through. He had taken over in the emergency.

"Not to worry, Jo," said that incomparable man. "When the indicator drops to zero you'll still have about twenty gallons of petrol in the tanks. You'll make ten thousand with that. And get as far towards the coast as you can before you bail out. You can't make a crash landing in the muck that's down here."

"I could try," suggested Capka.

"It's up to you," said Ocelka. "I don't advise it."

The R.T. went dead as Capka came on the intercom.

"Well, chaps," he said, "you've heard it all. What do you want to do?"

He was, as usual, calm and in complete control of himself. Several voices at once sounded together.

"Crash land, skipper."

They knew their pilot. In their opinion he was second only to the "old man" himself. It would have broken their hearts to have to fly with anyone else. Now it looked as if more than their hearts were to be broken.

Then Capka was speaking again, to his navigator.

"What are your views, Mr. Karel?"

Capka, like Jan and Josef, always called Karel Lancik "Mister" in deference to his commissioned rank—three officers and three sergeants made up the crew of "C" for Cecilia.

"Oh, try crash landing," said Lancik, imperturbable as ever. "Honington's only five miles away. You know the place like the palm of your hand."

"Good enough," said Capka.

Josef's excited voice broke in.

"There's a Stirling to starboard and they've all jumped."

"They must have received the same advice as us," said Capka calmly, adding, "Give me the heading for Honington, Mr. Karel."

The warning lights on the pilot's instrument panel began to flicker. The petrol tanks were rapidly emptying.

"087," came Lancik's reply almost on the instant.

"Right," said Capka. "087 it is. It will be a rough landing, so brace yourselves, everybody, and Jan, hold Antis in your lap. And, all of you, as soon as I land get out as fast as you can."

"I can't get Honington," said the co-pilot, a moment later. "Try them through East Wretham."

The Wing Commander was still in control at the Watch Office.

"I'm going to try and land at Honington," said Capka. "We can't get them————."

"All right. We'll get in touch."

The seconds passed. Jan would have been surprised if there were now enough petrol in the tanks to moisten a handkerchief. The Wing Commander came through to them again.

"Honington's unserviceable, but they'll do what they can. Watch out for a 'red' at the beginning of the only runway that you can use. Good luck!"

Then Capka spoke once more on the intercom:

"I'm going down. Brace yourselves, and get hold of the dog, Jan."

Jan groped his way aft, picked up Antis, and hugged him close to him with both arms. He wished that he could interpose his body between the dog and whatever might come.

At five hundred feet he saw the amber glow of a flashing beacon and at the same time the two red Very lights floating in mid-air to port. The dark and shadowy shapes of hangars loomed through the fog. Then he could see the runway racing past beneath and they were down.

5

Antis was twice wounded on operations. Over Kiel a fragment of shrapnel scraped his nose and lacerated his left ear, which acquired a permanent droop. The splinter finally lodged in Jan's flying boot. At the same time he cut his paw.

In mid-August, in an attack on Hanover, a shell exploded directly under "C" for Cecilia, capsizing her as she turned for home. Showers of splinters penetrated the fuselage, but the engines were unharmed. Later, on the same trip, they were coned by searchlights and attacked by night fighters, but escaped into cloud. When they reached home the undercarriage was found to be jammed and they were forced to belly-land. Antis, wounded four hours previously, lying in a pool of his own blood, had remained quietly at his master's feet. He was found to have a three-inch gash in his chest.

Immediately on landing Jan rushed the dog to Station Sick Quarters, where he was operated upon. Thereafter Antis was grounded and barred the airfield. The dog resented the restrictions, but Ludva, himself just back from hospital, was able to look after him. Moreover, while "C" for Cecilia was being patched up "U" for Ursula replaced her. As the pitch of the latter's engines was unfamiliar, Antis suffered little anxiety. And during his convalescence he made a new friend. She was blonde, petite, and charming. A deep affection swiftly developed between the two. Her grandmother—"Mother Brown" to the Czechs, who had grown fond of the old lady—kept a grocery shop in the village. The name of Antis' friend was Jacqueline, and she was four years of age.

Jan "briefed" Antis on his new assignment. The dog was fully aware that the child was committed to his care and that he was responsible for her safety.

Every morning the two met and walked towards the meadow where they played, the child toddling alongside her escort with her fingers held fast in his collar. When they crossed the road the dog would wait with pricked ears until he was satisfied that no traffic was approaching and only then make the passage.

At times Jacqueline, in search of kingcups and daisies to make a chain to adorn her devoted admirer, would wander near the stream that flowed through their preserve. Then the dog would advance upon the child and, ignoring her protestations, seize her by the skirt, and drag her to safety.

Nobody would attack Jacqueline as long as Antis was with her. And Antis and Jacqueline were concerned with nobody but themselves.

The last trip of Jan's tour was to Berlin. "C" for Cecilia with her crew safe and sound—they were indeed the first Czech crew to survive a tour intact—completed this last mission successfully, though the aircraft was severely damaged. So, with the tour at an end, Jan prepared for fourteen days' leave. He had completed two hundred and six operational flying hours in forty-one trips, and Antis thirty-two hours in seven trips.

Both man and dog had been wounded. The next move after their leave would be to the new Czech depot at R.A.F. St. Athan, with Jan in the rank of Flight Sergeant.

They went to Wolverhampton near Cosford for their leave. And so for fourteen blissful days they walked the countryside again and both were in good company.

Pamela was glad Jan's tour was over, but on his return to East Wretham, Jan himself was not so sure. Faced with imminent departure, his heart ached.

He said good-by to Adamek and his ground crews. They were all inarticulate with the distress of parting and the news that "C" for Cecilia on her return to duty had been shot down with the loss of her entire new crew.

Then he went to Ocelka's office, and the Wing Commander waved aside Jan's thanks, patted Antis, wished them both the best of luck and sent them on their way. At "Mother Brown's" shop in the village there were further good-bys and good wishes. Jacqueline clung round Antis' neck with tears. And with all that over, there was the Thetford bus to catch and a last farewell to the villagers of East Wretham, who stood in their doorways or at their garden gates. Then lastly there was Ludva, waiting to see them off and deciding to travel with them to the station.

When they said good-by on the platform, Jan could scarcely bear to look Ludva in the face and the grip of their hands was almost like that of drowning men.

Then Jan said in a strangled voice, which was meant to be lighthearted:

"So long, Ludva. See you in London at Christmas with the rest of the chaps. So long."

Then Antis and Jan were in the train and on their way. Neither of them was ever to see Ludva again.

1

Jan was aghast at the news his roommate Cupak had just phoned from St. Athan. Cupak was taking care of Antis while Jan, at the Central Gunnery School, was waiting for a permit to keep Antis at the school at Chelveston. But now he didn't know what to do.

Cupak had reported that, while he was walking with Antis this morning, the dog had taken off after a flock of sheep. Almost immediately Cupak had heard a shot and seen the dog stagger. A second shot had followed, which bowled Antis over. He had picked himself up and made his way back to camp, limping badly. Shortly afterwards a farmer had arrived on the scene with a shotgun. He stated that Antis had already killed three of his sheep, that he was reporting the matter to the Commanding Officer, Group Captain Davies, and that, as well as compensation, he wanted the dog shot. He had then taken Cupak's name.

The dog's eye was badly cut, Cupak continued, and at Station Sick Quarters they had extracted thirty-six pellets out of his hide. Cupak was still poulticing the eye on the Medical Officer's advice, but the Station Commander had ordered him to shut the dog up except for two periods of exercise a day, until the case came before the court at Cowbridge. He was now in the guard room. Wing Commander Shepherd, who admired Antis, was loath to believe that the dog was that most shameful thing, a sheep-killer, but Cupak had felt bound to admit that, though he had not seen Antis pull down a victim, he had nevertheless seen him chasing sheep. The farmer was demanding full satisfaction. This was the ugly news that Cupak passed over the telephone, concluding with an appeal to Jan to apply for leave to be present when the trial came up at the County Court.

He applied for leave but, as the course was only beginning, his application was refused.

He was in despair. If his dog were a killer he must pay the penalty. It was no good at all arguing on the score of human moralities. He had treated Antis like a fellow human, but the fact remained that Antis was a dog. He was loyal and companionable and in many ways worthy of praise, but in his world it was natural for certain animals to pursue and hunt and kill. It was not fair to expect a moral code from them. Antis could well be a killer.

It was like discovering that a twin brother was a murderer!

And Antis, his once trusted and beloved friend and dearest possession, was already in the condemned cell and he wasn't allowed to go to him.

In his desperation, he wrote to Group Captain Pickard by express letter, imploring his help. The answer came back by telegram:

WILL DO WHAT I CAN. GOOD LUCK.

He had regretted sending the letter as soon as he had posted it, feeling that he had acted on impulse. But the Group Captain's reply gave him hope and raised his spirits, so that he became still more determined to stand by Antis.

He went down to the village inn on the following Tuesday evening in deep distress. Another call from Cupak had brought news that Antis was on the mend and his case was coming before the Court on Friday. Jan sat in his own corner of the bar. Feeling lonely, he began to explain to the man next to him something of his trouble. He knew in a very short time that this stranger with the mild brown eyes and drooping moustache was, of all people in the world, the very one he sought. He was a shepherd. In after days the only name that Jan ever remembered calling him was "Dai."

Encouraged by this new-found friend and only too grateful to unburden himself, he told the story of Antis from the beginning, and then his present trouble.

When he had concluded Dai spoke his piece. It was so much to the point that Jan at once grew sober and every word sank in, because these were words of wisdom, born of long experience.

"Nobody's ever seen this dog of yours worry sheep, you say?" said Dai.

"My friend only saw Antis chasing them. But the farmer claims three—"

"Ah, farmers!" said Dai. "They all want to make up their losses. It wouldn't be natural otherwise, would it, now?"

"That's true," agreed Jan.

"And sheep fetch a tidy price these days. I don't say the farmer's dishonest. He finds a dead sheep and he has his suspicions. It's only to be understood he wishes to pin it upon someone, is it not?"

"Yes," said Jan.

"Has your dog ever met with sheep much before?"

"I suppose he must have done, I don't really know. He's led a different life from lots of dogs."

"No dog ever worried sheep on his own."

"That's news to me," said Jan.

"There will be at least a pair of them. A killer won't hunt unless he has company."

"You mean," said Jan excitedly, "there's a killer dog in the first place and then the other dog joins in?"

"The bad dog leads astray his companion. He must have a friend to keep him company. It's an instinct that goes back God knows how far."

"Are you telling me that Antis was corrupted?"

Dai laughed. "Encouraged, let us call it! It is the bad dog that first shows the way."

"Then Antis needn't have done the actual killing?"

" 'Deed to God, it could well be so! Unless it were proved otherwise."

"My God!" said Jan. "This is an eye-opener! It shows what a fat lot I knew about dogs."

"Man, they're the study of a lifetime. You should see my Trix at work!"

"What shall I do?" said Jan. "They may shoot my dog."

"Never mind the big friends you are writing to. You must write to the Clerk of the Court. You must say who this dog of yours is and what he has done. Then you must point out what I have told you. And then, if no one will swear they have seen your dog actually worrying sheep, he may get off, though you may have to foot the bill."

"I think Antis may owe his life to you," said Jan. "I know I owe you my peace of mind."

Jan sat up all night writing his letter. When the Court considered the case on the following Friday, Jan was ordered to pay eleven shillings costs, compensation to the farmer to the tune of thirty-two pounds, and to keep the dog under proper control. But the dog's life was saved.

On the completion of the course and his return to St. Athan, Jan decided to teach the dog his lesson. It was clear that Antis had missed Jan. On two occasions the dog had broken camp to look for him. He had escaped from Cupak's room when its occupant was absent at breakfast by turning the handle of the door in his teeth—an old trick which Jan had taught him in order to get out at night on his own without disturbing anyone—and had been found at the local railway station, with which he was familiar, by an irate Wing Commander Shepherd. In the second instance he had gnawed through a strap fastening him to the leg of the bed, opened a window with a loose catch, and again making for the station, had boarded a train and been found by a Czech sergeant-pilot who knew him on the platform at Cardiff.

Both episodes had driven the unfortunate Cupak frantic with worry, since the dog was still under the jurisdiction of the Court and could have been shot. Cupak was even more delighted than Antis to see Jan back.

Within hours of his return Jan enlisted the aid of a neighboring farmer, who had not been involved in the previous trouble, but had heard of the case.

Jan led Antis to the middle of a field in which a flock of thirty Welsh mountain ewes were in full sight. He ordered the dog to "sit," and left the meadow, keeping Antis under observation. Four hours later, Jan recalled Antis.

At no time did Antis attempt to molest the flock. Jan repeated the treatment for three days in succession, and Antis remained quiet and obedient the whole time. If, indeed, a lesson had been necessary, it had been well and truly learned. From that moment to the end of his days Antis disregarded the presence of sheep.

But it was to Jan's profound regret that his posting in May of 1942 to No. 8 Air Gunnery School at Evanton in north Scotland as an Instructor came through before he could encounter Dai again and assure him that he had not only saved the dog's life but, most important of all, had restored his master's faith in him.

2

It was late spring when Jan reported to Evanton in north Scotland. The small camp lay in a Highland valley, shielded on the north by Cnoc-Fyrish, one of the great range of mountains. On the southern border lay Cromarty Firth. The woods at the edge of camp teemed with wild life, rabbits and badgers and foxes. If it brought back to Jan memories of his own country, to Antis it was paradise.

He became rapidly popular with the young air gunners. He would rouse sluggards at reveille each morning, bounding on a bed and dragging off the blankets. When Jan went into Inverness to dance or visit the cinema, the trainees would tease and play with him.

There was, indeed, too much friendliness. Jan, relieved of the strain of operational flying, unconsciously slackened his discipline. Antis began to exhibit signs of marked disobedience. He strayed into Inverness in search of Jan and became lost, arriving on the wrong bus at Dalcross instead of Evanton. He was brought back next day in a Botha on a training flight. After the escapade, Jan punished him by completely ignoring his presence.

In October he won a dog show at Dingwall, and the leading Scottish papers printed his story with photographs. He was becoming so spoiled that Jan could no longer leave him with friends. Once he discovered his master at a dance in the Town Hall and tore the dress of Jan's partner, whom he imagined to be attacking his master. There were other incidents, trivial enough in themselves, but straws in a wind which was to reach gale force.

In September 1942, Jan was commissioned and moved across to the officers' mess. The work in the Air Gunnery School continued; Jan lectured and flew, the daily routine became a matter of habit in a very peaceful existence.

And for Antis there was always the woods. He roamed at will but always returned. Or he would lie on the bank of the stream that flowed by the wood, watching the ducks that swam past. He made no attempt to molest them, and they, grown familiar with his presence, would swim within inches of his nose. The trees of the dark wood came down to the edge of the opposite bank, and beyond rose the magnificent heights of Cnoc-Fyrish.

Christmas passed and New Year's day came in bitterly cold with a darkened sky. It had started snowing in the morning in huge flakes that rapidly covered the ground. Jan went to his room soon after dinner, heaped up the stove with coal, and took a book from the shelf. Antis lay asleep at his feet. Dog and man had now been together for over three years.

The snow stopped falling by ten o'clock. Jan had dozed off, but awoke suddenly to a distinct, insistent sound that permeated his dream. It was the far-off howling of a dog. Antis too was listening.

Then Antis, who had been restless for several days, rose to his feet and crossed to the door. He stood, ears forward, body tense. Jan rose and opened his door to let the dog out for his nightly run. As Jan followed him out into the corridor, he saw the bright moonlight through the open door at the end.

Antis suddenly lifted his head and bayed, a considerable noise in that confined space. Then in a flash, he was out of the hut and racing over the moonlit snow.

Jan's whistles were useless. Somewhere on Cnoc-Fyrish, at the mouth of her den, a bitch was waiting for a mate.

Antis was gone in the hills for five days and nights. A further snowfall made deep and dangerous drifts. Jan refused all offers of help, for he knew a search would be useless. He was told the story of a wild Alsatian bitch, born from a mother who had taken to the hills. Antis was under a greater spell than he had ever known before.

No animal brought up in civilized circumstances could survive the hardships of a Highland winter. By the end of the fifth day, Jan gave up Antis for lost. But concern in the dog's fate was widespread. Six airmen returning to lectures after lunch on the sixth day immediately recognized Antis trotting towards the village.

They made a concerted dash to capture him. Alarmed, the dog careered down the lane and leapt a low iron fence. He missed his footing and was impaled on two of the iron spikes that decorated the top. It was only with considerable difficulty that he was extricated.

He was badly hurt. A spike had penetrated the stomach. Jan rushed the dog into Inverness to a veterinary surgeon. His diagnosis was alarming. It was doubtful if Antis would live, but there was a bare chance if he was operated on at once. With no other course to pursue, Jan left the dog and made his way back to camp.

On the following afternoon with the help of Flying Officer Ziegler, who agreed to take his lectures, Jan returned to Inverness. Antis was still alive but very ill. On the fourth day he was still very weak and needed careful nursing, but could be removed.

Jan took the dog back to camp, and with the aid of the Medical Officer, Antis survived.

In the first week of June, Jan surprised Antis, now recovered, on the far side of the stream that flowed past the camp. It had never been the dog's custom to cross over the stream where the tall trees fringed the bank. Something was occupying his attention. Unobserved, Jan sat down on the near bank to watch.

Antis lay at the edge of the wood, his forelegs stretched out before him as he lay on his stomach, but his hind quarters slightly raised as if to spring. His ears were cocked, his head erect and a little on one side. Every now and again he would advance his forepaws an inch or two and slither his belly along the ground. The attitude was the familiar invitation to play.

Something was moving in the undergrowth at the foot of the trees. Each time it started to emerge Antis shifted his position. Once he barked and the creature hastily disappeared, only to partially disclose itself at another point. Then once again the game would continue.

Jan knew that it could not be a rabbit, but it was clearly wild. Yet no fox or badger would have remained in the presence of its natural enemy. Whatever was attracting the dog's attention was obviously itself attracted in turn. It was becoming impossible for Jan to resist joining in the fun. He was about to whistle softly when the mysterious object revealed its identity.

It was a three-month-old Alsatian puppy.

Jan made his presence known. There were in Jan's pocket scraps of biscuit for Antis. He crossed the stream and sat down by his dog. The puppy at once retreated, but in a little time returned peering out of the bracken with inquisitive, bright eyes. Jan flicked a scrap of biscuit towards it and remained motionless. After a long pause the puppy emerged and licked the scrap. Jan laid a restraining hand on Antis. The dog was trembling with excitement. In half an hour's time the ground was littered with fragments of biscuit and the puppy was in the open. Jan reached out a cautious hand. The puppy scuttled back into the shelter of the trees. Though they waited till the sun sank, they saw no more of the little creature.

And though on subsequent occasions Jan took Antis to the identical spot, the puppy was never seen again.

3

In November 1944, Jan, in the rank of Flight Lieutenant, rejoined No. 311 Squadron, now at Tain, flying Liberators as a Radio and Radar Operator for a second tour of operations.

The Evanton School closed down in October 1943. It had, on the whole, been a happy time, with many friends in the district. Antis had by now recovered from his injury. From Evanton, Jan went to teach at Pembray, and then studied radar at Cranwell. Now at Tain he was back with his old Squadron engaged in antisubmarine patrols and occasional daylight strikes against the German Navy in the Baltic. Very few of the original air crew remained, but the administrative staff and ground crews were almost identical, with Adamek in charge of Jan's aircraft and Kubicek now a corporal.

It was a bitterly cold winter in the north of Scotland, and Antis had reverted to his original habit of keeping vigil when Jan was operating. It had been of no avail shutting the dog in his room, because he kept everyone awake with his nightlong howls. The only place where he would remain quiet was at Adamek's tent. The station tailor made a coat from a blanket for him. Antis liked the coat. As soon as Jan picked up his flying kit the dog would seek out his coat and carry it to his master to put on. Then both would go on duty together, Jan to operate over the Arctic Ocean, and Antis to watch the sky for his master's return. The coat succeeded in keeping the dog warm when the winter weather was moderate, but now that the December cold had set in the long hours of vigil were beginning to prove exacting, since they lasted from twelve to fifteen hours. Antis invariably shared the hot meal provided for air crews after their operational report.

In the second week of December, during a patrol on which Jan was engaged, the weather closed in with fog. Jan's aircraft was diverted to the Shetlands, but back at Tain, Antis, out in the perimeter, still kept watch. In the early hours of the morning two of Jan's friends, fearing that the dog might die of exposure, drove out, picked him up, and wrapping him in a blanket, took him back to their quarters. After rubbing him down and placing him before a roaring fire in their hut they waited with him until he slept. It was the first occasion Antis had permitted anyone to interfere with his vigil.

By dawn the weather cleared, and Jan landed at Tain the following day. He immediately inquired after his dog. Adamek told him what had happened.

"Flight Lieutenant Vaverka and Flight Lieutenant Rybar took him away," said Adamek. "He was in a bad state. I've never known him to allow strangers to touch him before. It was just like that time at East Wretham. Do you remember that? If it hadn't been for the Padre I don't know what we'd have done."

"Yes, I remember," said Jan with some feeling.

He could hear again the voice of a man now dead. "Hostages to fortune," the voice was saying, "I'll always look after the dog for you if anything happens." But Ocelka was in his grave and many of those around him now were comparative strangers. And he thought again as he had long ago, "God knows what the end will be."

Then he hurried to Antis. The dog was very ill. His eyes were glazed and his breathing labored. He rallied at the sight of his master but refused to eat, and drank inordinately. On the next day he began to pass blood.

Jan took him to the veterinary surgeon in Tain.

The dog's kidneys were diseased and had weakened his bladder. He should never be locked in where he could not get out. He could die at any time, but with careful treatment could last for years. The greatest danger of all lay in exposure to excessive cold. Another such occasion as the recent one could kill him.

Jan went back to Tain and held a council of war with four fellow officers, Rybar, Vaverka, Hering, and Dolezal. The subject of the council of war, still weak from his experience, dozed by the stove.

"If Antis isn't broken of the habit of waiting for me," said Jan, "he's as good as dead already."

"I've got nothing to suggest," said Hering.

"When I was at Evanton," said Jan, "the trainees used to play with Antis in my absence. And I was away often. I used to get annoyed with the trainees, but now————"

"Are you suggesting," said Rybar, "that if you encourage Antis to take orders from other people and allow them to handle him as Vaverka and I did the other night, that he'll begin to lose interest in you?"

"I can't see any other way out," said Jan. "The dog's life's at stake."

"Without his love for you," said Rybar wisely, "he wouldn't have any life."

"If I get diverted again," said Jan, "it can easily be for more than a matter of twenty-four hours. It's midwinter and there are weeks of it yet to come."

"I'll give a hand," said Dolezal. "You tell us what you want us to do, and we'll give it a trial."

"That goes for me," said Hering, and Vaverka agreed.

"I'll come in too," said Rybar, "but only under protest."

Vaverka reached out and stroked the dog. Antis stirred and his tail twitched.

"You poor old so-and-so," said Vaverka softly. "We've got to try and help you break your heart."

"It'll never work," said Rybar. "But one can only try."

"I think it a sound idea," said Dolezal.

"I suppose," said Rybar, "that we've got the right to do this."

And then, because he saw the sudden acute distress on Jan's face, he got to his feet and pressed the bell for a mess waiter.

"Let's have a drink," he suggested. "We're with you, Jan, for what it's worth."

On the very next morning Jan picked up his hat and coat to go for a walk. Antis at once rose and picked up his master's gloves in the old familiar and engaging self-taught trick. Jan snatched the gloves from him and ordered him back to his bed in the stern tone of voice which he used when the dog did wrong. Antis, bewildered but obedient, slunk back to his couch. Jan strode out of the room, slamming the door behind him. He left the dog gazing after him, hurt and disconsolate.

Jan tramped through the snow for three long hours, sick at heart and ashamed. The eternal barrier of the spoken word was forcing him to betray his friend. In all times of despair, a stranger in a strange land, with all the strain of operational flying, and with extinction always around the corner, there always had at all times been one comforter who had never failed. In hours of loneliness and longing he had unburdened his heart to his dog. There was no good saying that Antis didn't understand. He had never failed to appreciate a mood. There had been no shame in tears before Antis, nor dread of betrayal. And now that faithful heart must be broken because no explanation was possible.

And he thought as he tramped through the snow, how right Ocelka had been and how his own desperate need for love had brought both himself and his dog to this tragic impasse. He condemned himself for his own thoughtless selfishness and longed to return and comfort his friend. But he kept on, because the task must be completed.

When he returned, Antis was still on his blanket. He rose eagerly, but Jan ordered him back to his bed and turned his back on him. The dog obeyed, his misery and bewilderment woefully apparent.

On the following day Jan purposely moved into a larger hut with his four friends and five other fellow officers, reluctantly persuaded to join the plot. Antis, who had always slept beside his master, was given a bed in the center of the room by the stove. On each occasion that Jan entered and the dog rose to greet him, he was peremptorily ordered back to his couch.

At noon Jan made no attempt to invite Antis to the check-up for the night's patrol. In his absence one of his roommates picked up the dog's brush to groom him. His efforts were greeted with an ominous growl. Rybar brought Antis his food. Jan gave Antis his medicine and then went out. His food was still untouched when Jan departed for his mission with no word of farewell.

But that night the weather closed in again and Jan's aircraft was diverted once more to the Shetlands.

It was two days before the Liberator landed at Tain. Dolezal broke the news to Jan.

The plan had failed. Antis had refused to eat, nor had he allowed anyone to take him out for exercise. It had been impossible to give him his medicine.

"I shouldn't have believed it," said Dolezal. "But there it is. If you want to persist in this idea you'll have to do it alone. We are all sick of seeing the dog suffer. Without you he will die."

"We tried everything," said Vaverka, "if you'd not got back today we should have had to hand him over to the vet."

"We're sorry," said Rybar, "but we're through. If we had taken the dog into Tain I'm perfectly certain the vet would have put him out of his misery."

Jan went to his hut. Antis lay curled up on the blanket. His eyes were open and he was still breathing, but he showed no other signs of life. Jan knelt down beside him and took his dog's head in his lap. The glazed eyes showed no recognition.

"I'm back," said Jan, "the bloody fool that calls himself your master is back. Wake up, wake up, I'm back."

Antis tried to lift a paw. Jan took him in his arms.

"That sort of loyalty and devotion," said Rybar, "is something that no one can break."

"It's all my fault," said Jan, brokenly.

"It's more than any of us deserve," said Vaverka softly, "but I could wish it were me, nevertheless."

"Don't die," pleaded Jan to his dog. "Don't leave me, boy." Then someone fetched some porridge in a bowl, and someone else poured cream over it. The dog's throat was parched and dry, but Jan spoon-fed him till the bowl was empty. Then Antis slept.

For three days Jan nursed his dog. The vet came over from Tain and between them they pulled Antis around. He recovered towards the end of their ministrations remarkably quickly. In a little time his strength and vigor returned.

With the coming of spring he no longer kept vigil in Jan's absence. After take-off he would trot away happily with his friends. On June 2, 1945, while patroling the coast of Norway, the Liberator in which Jan flew received its final recall to base.

For man and dog the war was at an end.

4

August 15, 1945, was an exceptionally fine day. With Antis at his feet, Jan, in company with the other eleven Liberators of No. 311 Squadron, flew over Germany. There was no opposition from 'flak' nor fighters. The Squadron was on its way home.

There had been some delay in repatriation, but at length, agreement had been reached with the Russians, who had claimed the liberation of Czechoslovakia. Thereafter the entire Squadron had been detailed to attend a course of Russian.

But now, at last, they were going home.

As they approached the western frontier of Czechoslovakia a formation of twelve Spitfires met them as escort. In Prague the bands were playing and the crowds cheering. The hour for which the exiles had waited and endured was at hand. As Jan climbed out of his aircraft at Ruzyn airdrome a girl of golden beauty embraced him. He had never seen her in his life before, but it occurred to him that, with Antis prancing beside him, there could be no more fitting a welcome home.

Home! He was home! His dog was still with him and they were both alive. And the name of the girl who kissed him was Tatiana. . . .

chapter i   *"May I Offer You a Vodka?"*

1

Jan supposed that he should have realized that everything might have worked out this way from the moment they had flung the conductor off his bus outside Ruzyn airdrome. Now, three years later, as he rode along in this disreputable car fleeing toward freedom, he remembered the hilarious sight of the conductor sprawling in the gutter with the Red Star pinned to his bottom. The jubilant young hero returned that day from the war had no foreboding of exile so soon again.

The conductor had been Jan's first experience with Communist domination. He had refused to allow the bus to move unless Jan removed Antis. Jan had kept his temper, but the other passengers had finally unended the man in the gutter. They, too, were unused to the new officiousness. Today no one would dare such behavior.

The years following had been so blissfully happy and successful that they must have blinded him to what was taking place in his cherished world. He had married his golden girl Tatiana, and they lived in a magnificent flat suitable for a Captain of the Czech Air Force working at the Ministry of National Defense. Jan's friend, Jan Masaryk, the Minister of Foreign Affairs, was godfather to their son Robert. Jan had become a successful author, with three books about the war and his comrades, and many articles and plays to his credit. Antis, through these, was famous too.

Jan ached now with longing at the thought of that enchanted life, vanishing behind him, perhaps forever. He had not been able to say a special farewell to Tatiana, for he was sworn not to tell her of his doom.

But she had been as aware as he of peril since February 1948, when the Red Government began to declare everyone who had associations with the West as suspect. For the Czech ex-R.A.F. personnel, the future became particularly hazardous, as they were accused of the "crime" of assisting the Western Powers during the war. Jan's publications became evidence against him. Two Stalinist officers had been installed in his office, friendly, but unquestionably, spies. The flat was also under observation, and their friends stayed clear of it.

The menace of arrest had increased until the morning, seven weeks ago, when Masaryk had sent for Jan and warned him that he headed the Communist black list. He must leave Czechoslovakia. And he must not tell Tatiana. Masaryk had also told Jan that his chief at the Ministry of Defense, Colonel Vacek, was high on the purge list.

Three days later, the Communists had announced the suicide of Dr. Masaryk. Rumor said it was no suicide; the purge had begun in earnest. That was on March 10. It was not until April 27 that the blow had fallen on Jan. The O.B.Z., whose Russian equivalent was the N.K.V.D., had sent for him. His writings were spread out on the table before five inquisitors. The censor may have passed them for publication last year, they said; this year they were treasonable. True friends of the State did not glorify the British. He was to write about the Russian Air Force only. Furthermore, he was to report—and encourage— any criticism of the State made by his friends at the Air Force Club.

They held out a folded blue paper, explaining that it was a warrant for his arrest which would be in force on Friday, the thirtieth, if he did not agree to these terms.

"That is all, Captain Bozdech," the voice continued to echo in his ear, as if it were in a far-off dream.

Today is Friday the thirtieth, he thought, jouncing in the car on the rough road, and by now they know. By now, Tatiana knows. He thought of her, a soldier's daughter, standing dry-eyed with Robert in her arms. But she would be safe with her parents. He could not have done anything else. Much better for her to be a temporary grass-widow than a widow in fact with no hope for their future together. No option remained to him but to flee the country.

He had walked the streets with Antis most of the night trying to figure out how this was to be done, but without success. In the morning on his way to work, an acquaintance blundered into him and whispered quickly:

"Tonight at eight. Café Pavlova Kavarna at Strahove. The password is 'May I offer you a vodka?' "

Jan's hopes soared. The underground was working for him. Escape was possible.

2

The Café Pavlova Kavarna was a commonplace little restaurant in a typical Prague suburb. Three other men were in an upstairs room to meet Jan. They had been preparing the links in the chain of his and Vacek's escape. Their information about the events and people in the government was astonishingly accurate, and they had given Jan his instructions quickly.

He was to become a peasant up from the country with a knapsack of butter to sell. After he had left his office, the following day, Thursday, he would go to a lavatory in a public square where an attendant would have his peasant clothes. He would change there, leaving his uniform with the attendant. Then he would go to a certain farm on the outskirts of the city where a car would be waiting for him.

He was to pass on the instructions to Vacek who would do exactly the same thing as he ten minutes later.

The next morning it had been difficult to keep his voice steady and his manner as casual as if he were leaving for the ordinary day's routine. He said a good-by to Tatiana and kissed the baby in her arms. When the door had closed behind him, it had been like a blow to the heart; he had stood for a moment almost winded with agony, longing to cast caution aside and return. But he had managed to pull himself together and move resolutely on his way.

One thing was certain: Antis must go with him. He could not be separated from his dog as well as from his wife and child. He had evolved a plan. When he got to the office, he had told his clerk Frantisek Vesely to make an appointment with the animal hospital. The dog's nails had to be clipped. Tatiana had been complaining that Antis was ripping her carpet. Then he had sent Frantisek to the flat to get Antis and bring him to the office for Jan to take him to the veterinarian. This would make sense to Tatiana and explain his absence to his office spies. With luck, he would get a flying start, he had felt, and Antis would be with him. And this was the way it had worked out, perfectly, without a hitch.

He had changed clothes and found the farm without difficulty. He had waited pleasantly in the sweet hay in the barn until Vacek came to join him in the two-ton van waiting outside with its driver. At the end of an hour and a half of steady driving, the van had drawn up alongside another car on the road and they had changed over to it.

Jan had thought that Vacek seemed unnecessarily nervous, and finally Vacek had admitted that there was trouble in Prague having nothing to do with Jan that he could not explain. And indeed, at the next change of cars, there was a message for Vacek which made him decide to return to Prague. Jan instantly offered to accompany him, but Vacek refused. He said that Jan could not help him; that he would send a message somehow to let Jan know whether to wait for him or not. Then Vacek drove off the way they had come, waving to Jan through a window. Jan was never to see him again.

By dark, he had reached a village near the border and the farm of Vaclav Kaspar. Jan and Antis slept on the straw in the loft of his stable, exhausted with the events of the day.

He had awakened this morning thinking, "It is Friday," and instantly envying Antis, totally free of any foreboding, as he watched at a rat hole. During breakfast in Kaspar's kitchen a telegram had arrived to let Jan know that Vacek could not join him. Saddened, he had listened to the farmer's instructions.

He was to go to Anton's cottage, an hour's drive away. Kaspar only had known the first name of the man who would guide Jan across the border—"the greatest patriot of us all." He explained that none of them knew very much about their fellow collaborators. The over-all plan was never disclosed to any one individual. "If one is caught, there are ways of extracting information."

Jan marveled at the steady confidence of these patriots of all kinds, from the lavatory attendant to the owner of a huge farm, who, scorning reward or recognition, were ready to risk their freedom and their lives as long as they played a part, however small, in frustrating the aims of a regime loathed beyond the power of death itself.

A small lorry had stopped for Jan at Kaspar's farm, and after the hour's ride had left him at a cottage almost hidden by hedge and trees. Anton, a tall, bearded, sunburned man, had not been pleased when he saw Antis. Jan thought of the conversation.

"What do you want to bring a dog for?"

"Where I go, he goes with me," Jan had said.

"Wherever you go, he goes with you," repeated Anton. "Does that include hell? My God! Some of you people! Do you think that this is a picnic?"

And Jan had replied, "But this dog is trained. He's as good as a police dog."

"You can leave him behind," said Anton.

"Then I'd better make my way back," said Jan.

"The alarm's been raised in Prague," said Anton. "You might get a warm welcome on your return."

"I found this dog," Jan said, "as a puppy near the Siegfried Line nine years ago, and he flew with me over Germany with the Royal Air Force. He's better than another pair of eyes and ears on a job like this. I'm not going to desert him now after all we've been through together."

"Well," Anton had said, beginning to smile, "I think I like that." He had called Stefan Novotny, who had been waiting for three days for Anton to guide him across the border. Stefan had liked Antis immediately, and Anton's permission had been granted. Anton had brought some bread and milk and then revolvers for each of his companions. He had drawn a map on the ground explaining their route: through a forest, over a valley and on to the village of Kesselholst half a mile over the border in the American zone. Patrols, he said, changed check points frequently, and there was no telling what surprises were in store. The most dangerous part of the journey was in crossing the two hundred yards of valley between the forest and the frontier. He wanted to reach the far side of the forest by dusk.

Within ten minutes they were on their way in this mud-caked contraption which Jan had been so certain would break down.

1

Then he had realized that the ancient car with the spare iron shoe of a plough roped on to the back, and apparently four laborers aboard was all part of the plan. Now they had left the rough rutty tracks, and were rattling across open fields. In the late afternoon sunlight, the forest loomed before them.

The driver applied his brakes and they clambered out, with the dog at their heels. The car left them immediately.

The dense forbidding forest stretched from east to west in a solid belt of trees, as far as the eye could see. Only in places was the outline broken against the sky, where a track ran into the heart of the woods. To none of these arteries did Anton lead his companions. He plunged straight into the undergrowth, and Antis, who had known and loved the tangled recesses of another dark wood at the foot of Cnoc-Fyrish, forged ahead on Jan's instructions.

They struggled onward in silence, straining their ears for the slightest sound. When at times the undergrowth cleared Jan sent his dog on twenty yards ahead with the order to "seek," and Antis excelled himself. In a little while Anton whispered to Jan that he was glad that Antis was with them. Jan knew that no higher compliment could be paid.

Twice during three hours of walking, or crawling on hands and knees, the three men flung themselves to the ground at the dog's sudden signals of alarm. Twice Antis stopped dead, growling a warning and seconds later they too had heard faintly and far-off the snapping of twigs, and a distant voice, and once, the click of a rifle bolt.

At last, exhausted and aching, their flesh torn and smarting from thorn and bramble, they reached the northern limit of the forest and, lying prone, saw before them a wide and gentle valley ranged on the opposite side by the high wooded hills that lay between them and Kesselholst. A quarter of a mile away lay freedom, but down below in the drowsing valley lurked sudden death.

They saw the road and the turbulent stream and knew that river and road and silent valley were being steadfastly watched and that the sleepy and deserted countryside could suddenly bristle with hostility. They must wait for night.

It seemed to Jan that darkness would never fall. When the last gleam faded the sound of the curfew bell from Kesselholst echoed across the valley. It was the signal to keep the people and their cattle safely home. But it could, he felt, have been a knell that marked the passing, not only of a day, but of living souls such as himself. He wondered who tolled the bell, secure across the frontier, and how many other fugitives lay waiting for darkness before making the final desperate bid for freedom.

And he thought of the city he had abandoned and of Vacek, of Tatiana and his son. He wondered if the police had already called. Then darkness fell.

Across the valley, the lights of Kesselholst began to appear. The night became very silent. He thought he could hear the murmur of the river. Then he heard Anton's voice in his ear.

"All right. We'll go."

They rose cautiously to their feet, leaving the fringe of the forest and stepping into the open. Antis, at heel, kept close to Jan's left leg. Ahead the lights of Kesselholst blinked through the pitchy darkness. They began to descend the slope. The ground was rough and broken, and trailing brambles plucked at their ankles. Somewhere near by somebody's foot caught a loose stone, and Antis growled. The three men dropped to the ground. Complete silence enveloped them.

Antis suddenly ceased panting and beneath his hand Jan could feel the sinews of the dog's neck contract and the beginnings of another growl vibrate his throat. He tightened his warning grip. All was silence. The night flowed around them.

He was about to suggest a sudden dash for the frontier to Anton when he heard a footstep. It was quite distinct and unmistakable. Then he heard another, and another. He dug his fingers into Antis' coat and pressed himself flat to the ground. A long way off a train began to whistle as it passed behind the distant hills.

Then he saw the dark shapes of four men moving on his left.

A patrol, he was certain, had materialized appallingly out of the night. The sound of footsteps receded down the slope. He dared to breathe. And then, without warning, two searchlights split the night. One came from the west near the road, the other from the ridge before Kesselholst. They swept across the valley right and left, converged and separated, and crept together again. Then both beams swept up the slope towards the forest. They seemed to hover for the moment and then pounced unerringly on their prey. Four men scarcely fifty yards from Jan were racing for the trees. There was a sudden, devastating burst of machine-gun fire. Then the guns from a strong point directly ahead opened up.

All four men fell. Burst after burst was directed on the recumbent forms and the screams that had broken out on Jan's left ceased. As suddenly as it had started, the tumult died. The searchlights continued for fully a minute to sweep the slope and then the beam ahead of Jan flickered and went out. Only the one by the road remained, white and baleful, and fixed with an unwinking, dreadful intensity on the patch of ground the fugitives had crossed.

He lay frozen to the ground with Antis beside him and he knew that they owed their lives to the dog's timely warning. Now two service trucks sped into the valley and up the far slope. Jan could see four armed men in the leading vehicle.

The party alighted and, with the searchlight guiding them, made their way across the valley side. Two dogs trotted beside them. Soon could be heard their voices and laughter. Somebody called:

"There they are!"

And another voice:

"Well, it's the last time they will play that game!"

All were in army uniform, their rifles across their shoulders. They moved to and fro in the glare of the light. Now and again one of them would bend down and examine an object. One of the dogs came to a halt and sniffed.

"Leave him alone," said the sergeant. "He's not for dinner."

They all laughed uproariously. Jan thought: My countrymen! My God! What a world this is! His grip on Antis tightened, because the second dog, his head erect, with pricked ears, was coming towards him.

"We'll have to get transport," said the sergeant. "We can't carry these bastards all that distance."

He prodded a corpse with his toe. The other three began to shout to the car on the road. The second guard dog was drawing closer. Jan felt for his revolver.

"Come here, you," shouted one of the party. The dog trotted back to his handler.

They were half an hour collecting the bodies and loading them onto the car with shouts, laughter, and argument. At last both trucks drove off and darkness and silence settled on the valley again.

Anton crawled up between Jan and Stefan.

"This is the very devil," he whispered. "The way I intended to take is blocked by a new strong post. It wasn't here last time."

"What shall we do?" said Stefan. His teeth were chattering.

"We'll have to take an alternative route," said Anton. "It's not one I like. It's over the hill to the east of the river. It's pretty high, and we shall have to double back through the forest and make it under cover. We've only got five hours to daylight."

"And there's the river to cross," murmured Jan.

"Yes," said Anton grimly, "there's the river to cross. Let's go."

They crawled back to the forest on hands and knees, reaching the first of the trees with bleeding hands and bruised elbows. They rested a little and then began their passage through the wood. If it had been a torment in daylight, now in the darkness it was a nightmare. But their course was clear because they could hear the clamor of running water. At last, having crossed the road, they reached the bank of the river.

"We'll have to go farther downstream," said Anton. "It's too deep here."

They turned to their left. Antis kept close to Jan's side, and every now and then he would feel for the dog with an outstretched hand. When the bank began to descend Anton halted. Jan bumped against him in the darkness and Stefan behind stumbled into the dog.

"We'll try here," said Anton. "We can get down the bank."

They lowered themselves down, Anton first. Jan took Antis by the collar and found himself up to his knees in water. The strength of the current at once began to undermine the shingle beneath his boots.

"Now we link hands," said Anton. "The current gets stronger out there. But it's only twenty yards across."

"Take hold of my jacket," said Jan to his dog, and held out the tail of his coat. Antis took the cloth in his teeth.

"Now, hold tight," ordered Jan, and gave his left hand to Anton and the other to Stefan.

"Ready?" said Anton. "Let's go."

They edged their way foot by foot. The water reached their waists. Antis, his teeth fast in Jan's coat, started to swim. The river swirled and tugged at them. It was treacherous underfoot, and the stones gave way to their weight. Jan slipped and fell. The grip on each hand was immediately broken. He felt Stefan's fingers slip through his own, and though Anton clutched at his wrist, his hold gave way. Jan went down into the rushing water, dragging Antis with him and his forehead struck a boulder. He caught at the rock and found his fingers fast in a crevice. He plunged forward, tripped again, and felt his feet on the bottom. The current forced him askew as he flung his weight against it. He knew if he lost his precarious foothold that he would be swept downstream. He floundered towards the far bank till the water was up to his knees. He was drenched to the skin but still erect, and the pressure of the stream had slackened. He could feel the weight of the dog dragging at his jacket, but Antis was swimming strongly. Together they struggled up the bank and collapsed onto solid ground.

He lay for a little time, recovering his breath. There was no sign of his companions. He sat up and called, but the roar of the river drowned his voice. He called again louder, but there was still no answer. He dared not shout. The current could carry an unconscious man two score yards in less than a minute. Even if Anton were safe, the impenetrable night remained. Dawn could find them utterly lost and an easy prey. He groped in the dark and found the dog.

"Go! Seek!" he said insistently. "Seek! . . . *seek!*" Antis rose to his feet and disappeared into the darkness. The sound of the torrent stormed Jan's ears and senses. It seemed impossible to think coherently, but he knew that without Anton, daylight and death were synonymous. He wondered what folly had possessed him to dispatch his dog on so hopeless an errand. Then a blow in the back between the shoulder blades knocked the breath out of him. He gasped and clutched at his pocket for his revolver. A voice beside him began to curse. It was Anton's voice.

"Is that you?" said Jan, and felt the spray in his face as Antis shook himself. Then the dog's cold nose was on his cheek and the caress of a warm tongue.

"Thank God for the dog," said Anton. "I've got him by

the collar. I was washed away, but he found me and he's led me back to you."

Jan put out his hands and took Antis in his arms. His coat was dripping wet.

"Good boy," said Jan, and felt the quivering response of pride and pleasure.

His fingers found the back of the dog's ears and rubbed gently.

"Go, seek!" coaxed Jan again. Stefan, if he were still alive, must be found. Antis slipped from Jan's reach.

"There's a track round the hill," said Anton. "We can still make it, but I think they've felled trees to block the way. But we haven't much choice."

"We're in your hands," said Jan.

"And God's," added Anton.

There was a long pause. The roar of the river was thunderous.

"If Antis returns alone————?" said Jan, and left the question unfinished.

"Then we go on alone," said Anton. "Time's getting short." He stirred in the darkness.

"Your back's mighty hard," said Anton. "I hit it with my head. I was on my hands and knees holding onto the dog's collar."

There was the sound of labored breathing close at hand, followed by a footfall. Then came the low whine of the dog.

"Is Anton here?" said the voice of Stefan. "Is that you, Jan?"

"We're both here," said Jan.

Stefan dropped down beside them.

"I was swept downstream," he said, "into a pool. There was an overhanging branch. I was damn lucky. And then your dog found me. He's one hell of a good dog, isn't he? I think he saved my life."

"We must press on," said Anton. "Can you manage?"

"I shall be all right in a minute," said Stefan.

"The forest thins out," said Anton, "as the ground

rises, and farther on a path circles the crest. It comes out in a wood, a couple of hundred yards from the river, where it doubles back. Let's go."

They reached the western extremity of the forest within the hour, and began to climb. The stars became their guide.

But in a very short time they came to the first of the fallen trees. Lying horizontal to the ground with limbs untrimmed, each tree was a death trap. As Jan fought his way through the tangle of branches he wondered how many other entangled, exhausted fugitives had been discovered by a patrol and shot down. Finally their frenzied progress led to barren and rocky ground. And then the mist came down.

It swirled about them and the stars disappeared. It became impossible to see two paces ahead. But the dog ran from man to man, guiding and gathering and collecting them together. He herded them towards the crest. It was only when Anton, defeated by the mist, declared that even he was lost that Antis too relinquished his task. Despite the risk of a patrol stumbling upon them, they sank to the ground, huddled together in the shelter of a bush.

Jan sat with his arms round his dog and the warmth of the animal's body penetrated to him chilled in his saturated garments and in a little time he passed Antis over to Anton, and Anton, when he too had shared that precious warmth, passed the dog on to Stefan. So the dawn found them as the mist cleared. The long-sought path was only within a short pace of where they rested, and the crest of the hill was in sight.

They moved from the side of the path behind a giant boulder before making their final plan. Jan posted Antis on lookout on the top of the rock overlooking the path.

They would go, they decided, one at a time to the bottom of the hill, emerge from the sparse wood, and, racing full-tilt across the open valley, reach the river and cross. It was, so Anton declared, a plan that had succeeded at night more than once before. But now it was day-light and he had no idea what new observation posts or gun emplacement the Communists might have erected since he was last in the vicinity. It was a risk that must be run. As they rounded the hill freedom would be in sight.

"We will give it another half-hour before we start," said Anton. He broke a twig into two lengths to draw lots. As he held out his closed fist to Stefan, Antis suddenly growled. Then he leapt from the top of the boulder.

There was a clatter of falling stones, a wild stifled cry, and a savage snarling.

Revolver in hand, Jan ran round the rock with Stefan at his heels. Anton with his open knife was close behind.

A man in khaki uniform lay on his back across the path, his rifle useless beneath him and the bared teeth of the dog at his throat. There was nobody else in sight. Antis had already ripped the collar off the man's coat. The struggling, writhing seventy pounds of fury was something that Jan would never have recognized as his own dog. He grabbed Antis by the collar and dragged him clear. The prostrate man, with the wind knocked out of him, lay motionless, his terrified eyes goggling. He was one of the adolescent and brutal strong-arm fanatics with whom the Communists had replaced the original guards.

As soon as the dog, still snarling and snapping, had been dragged away, Anton had taken his place and the point of his knife was at the fellow's jugular vein.

"No," cried Jan. "No, Anton, not that."

"Why spare his life?" said Anton. "The swine deserves to die."

"Jan's right," said Stefan. "Not murder, Anton."

"You bloody fools," said Anton, but he got off the man's chest. They gagged him, then tied him up with strips slashed from his own shirt, and lashed him to a tree. Then, side by side, they ran round the hill with Antis bounding ahead of them. They entered the wood and reached the far side. The sun, in a cloudless sky, was rising over the ridge to the east before Kesselholst.

Two hundred yards of green meadow lay before them. In the middle of the meadow they saw a single hut. Telephone cables ran from its roof and on to the long line of posts running down the valley. An uncurtained window faced them and a shut door.

For fully an hour they waited. Nobody entered or left the hut. The early morning shadows down the valley shortened. A train chuffed its way up a distant gradient.

"Try the dog again," muttered Anton. Jan drew Antis to his side, pointed to the hut, and whispered in his ear. Then, with a final pat, he signaled the dog forward. The dog left them. He worked his way up wind to the hut and stood sniffing outside the closed door. Jan waved him on. The dog drew back on his haunches and barked. Three pigeons clattered out of a tree, but nobody came to the door.

"It's my belief," said Stefan, "that there was only one occupant to that hut and he's now tied to a tree."

"If I'd had my way———" Anton began.

But Jan was on his feet, his revolver in his hand. He was shaking with excitement. The moment had come to cast all caution aside.

"Come on," he cried and sprang out into the open.

At the sight of his master on his feet Antis raced towards him. Far off down the valley somebody shouted and then the three men with the dog leaping beside them were speeding across the meadow. They reached the bank of the river and plunged in. A dozen strokes in a smother of foam brought them to the opposite bank. It was low and shelving. They clambered up, panting and gasping. High reeds and withies rose before them. They ploughed their way through. Far behind them, in the still morning air, they could hear a telephone bell ringing violently from the hut in the meadow. The sound of a distant whistle reached them.

"On! On!" cried Anton.

An open field lay before them and beyond was a wood.

They ran like mad men for the sanctuary of the trees, and knew that at long last their pounding feet trod German soil.

2

They only slackened speed a mile from the border in sight of the village of Furth in Bavaria, within the Occupational Zone of the United States. Even so, they alarmed a farmer ploughing his field. Not three days previously, he told them, the Communist guards had pursued a man and his wife as far as this and shot them both out of hand.

They took the farmer's advice and reported themselves to the police station in Furth and claimed asylum. Then they handed over their weapons and received a hot meal and dry clothing, and were taken in a jeep to the United States base at Straubing, where they met three other Czech airmen, ex-R.A.F. officers, now fugitives like themselves. Anton, satisfied that his task was ended, bade them farewell. There were similar enterprises awaiting him. The escape route must be kept open.

Jan said good-by to this remarkable man, who claimed no reward for activities for which his life would be forfeit, with tears unashamedly in his eyes.

"Pray God," said Anton, "that we meet again in happier times. I was wrong about the dog, wasn't I? He was our salvation."

Then he wrung Jan and Stefan by the hand and departed.

The following day a further batch of fugitives brought news of Tatiana. A former fellow officer who had known Jan in Prague told him that all his property had been confiscated when his escape had become known and that his wife and child had sought refuge with her parents and were safe. Jan was heartbroken at the thought of his family but knew their decision had been the only one to take.

A fortnight later, having made known his decision to rejoin the R.A.F., Jan was removed in a party to a camp at Regensburg to await the necessary arrangements. The conditions at the transit camp were deplorable. For the majority there were no knives or forks and old tin lids scavenged from dustbins and refuse heaps served as plates, but Jan and his companions, warned of the conditions when at Straubing, had luckily been issued with cutlery, and a C.I.D. officer there, named York, had provided a large packet of dog meal for Antis. The dog, spoiled by the good food at the American base, refused to eat. Even the special dog meal failed to tempt him. Jan was obliged to spoon-feed him, mixing the meal into a thick porridge and forcing the unpleasant concoction down the dog's throat. Antis hated this undignified process, especially when it was carried out in public, so Jan found a ruined attic and fed the dog there. Antis, who had been looking thin and ill, soon regained his former vigor. He was a powerful swimmer, and a favorite evening pastime for Antis was to join Jan in swimming in the river near the camp.

Early in June, Jan was moved to Dieburg, near Frankfurt, and was housed with his companions in an old school building in a countryside of cornfields, whitewashed cottages, and orchards. Here nearly two hundred Czech refugees awaited passports for the free world.

The food and the accommodations still left much to be desired, but morale ran high, and the Camp Committee, headed by a Roman Catholic priest by name of Dobrovsky, did splendid work in making the life more bearable.

Jan and his friends were allocated to one room in which twelve-tier wooden beds occupied most of the space. Garments were scattered everywhere and any sort of privacy was impossible. With scarcely any room on the floor Antis slept on the bed below his master.

The Camp Committee could change only a very limited amount of Czech money, and the refugees were forced to live on the food provided by the camp. There was only spinach and a thick raisin soup, which Antis disliked.

With the dog meal now finished and refusing the soup, the dog began to lose weight and Jan was once again forced to spoon-feed him. At one time the food problem became so acute that an attempt to hunt wild pig in the adjacent woods was suggested. But after an unfortunate incident when Antis and Jan were nearly gored by a furious boar the idea was abandoned.

Early in July, Jan, with twelve others who wished to rejoin the R.A.F., was taken by lorry to Wiesbaden. They were medically inspected, passed fit, and issued with passports. On the terms of re-enlistment the Czech officers, including two ex-Wing Commanders and three ex-Squadron Leaders, found that they could not rejoin their old Service except in the lowest rank of A.C.2.

At the Hague, the port of embarkation, the Commanding Officer of No. 110 Movements Unit told Jan that it was impossible to take Antis to England without a permit from the British Ministry of Agriculture.

Jan refused to be parted from his dog, only to be told that if he refused to travel after re-enlistment, he could be posted as a deserter. Jan pleaded his cause and after a special signal to Air Ministry he was informed that, while he himself must travel immediately, steps were being taken to obtain the necessary permit for Antis. The officer in charge of No. 110 Movements Unit detailed one of his N.C.O.'s, Corporal Hughes, to look after the dog. The appearance of the corporal inspired both Jan and Antis with trust. As Jan handed over the lead he realized Hughes was one of those people who have a natural way with dogs, and when they walked along the quayside to the ship Jan kept beside the dog to give him confidence. Then he was on board with a last glimpse of Antis and Corporal Hughes as they stood watching from the dock.

On arrival in England Jan was posted to R.A.F. Cardington. Three weeks later Antis was in Hackbridge Kennels in Surrey for the requisite six months' quarantine. Every Wednesday and Saturday Jan visited the dog, but when in October he slipped a cartilage playing football and was unable to make the regular journey from Innsworth Hospital, the dog pined for him and became seriously ill. Once he attempted to escape, but the kennel wire was too strong and the concrete floor defeated his efforts to dig.

The dog grew worse. An urgent letter warned Jan that unless he could put in an appearance Antis would die. Jan was transferred from the rehabilitation center at Collaton Cross to Chessington, near Hackbridge, by courtesy of the medical authorities, and, though his leg was still in plaster, immediately called at the kennels.

Antis had become very ill indeed. His coat was lusterless and his eyes dim. But at the sound of the beloved master's voice—"Looking for someone?"—he whimpered and dragged himself to his feet and tried to offer a paw. After a time Jan persuaded him to eat and the dog relaxed, but on his master's departure he became so alarmed and distressed that only by leaving his gloves could Jan quiet him. It was the same old story that had repeated itself from the very beginning.

"He is getting old," said the veterinary surgeon in charge, "and he's in very bad shape now. All the symptoms indicate that he has not long to go. But you never know."

All the way back to the center at Chessington the words haunted Jan. He got off the bus when it arrived at its destination and found his way to the church. His distress was acute. It was a long time since Jan had prayed in a recognized place of worship, and the accepted words had slipped his memory. He felt like an intruder, coming cap-in-hand to beg of a charity to which he had seldom subscribed. But he repeated again and again words from his untutored heart. . . . "Spare him a little longer. . . . I am all on my own. . . . Please, just a few years more. . . ."

Antis was a little better the following day. He barked and his eyes were brighter and he had the strength to place his paws, as of old, on the kneeling man's shoulders, but almost at once another difficulty arose. Under the conditions of re-enlistment Jan had reverted to Air Crafts-man 2 from the wartime rank of Flight Lieutenant with the resulting loss of pay. It was now quite impossible to find the twenty-five shillings per week fees for the quarantine kennels. But after an urgent visit to London the People's Dispensary for Sick Animals, on learning the dog's history, came to the rescue and paid the fees.

In January 1949, his quarantine over, Antis was united again with Jan. The dog was now nine years old.

On March 14, 1949, his story became known through the People's Dispensary for Sick Animals. Antis was presented at the Ideal Home Exhibition at Olympia with the Dickin Medal, the Animal V.C., by Field Marshal Lord Wavell. He was the first non-British dog to win the award. In making the presentation Lord Wavell spoke as follows:

> I am just going to say a few words to the Dog. Dog Antis, it gives me great pleasure to make this presentation for "outstanding courage, devotion to duty and life-saving on several occasions while serving with the Royal Air Force and French Air Force from 1940-45 in England and Overseas," and devotion to your master. You have had many adventures by land and by air, and if you have not yet been in a naval battle it is only because you have not had the opportunity. You have been in action a great many times, and have been wounded, and you have inspired others by your courage and steadfastness on many occasions, and have been adopted as Mascot by your Squadron. You are the first foreign Dog to receive this award, which you have worthily earned by the steadfastness, endurance, and intelligence for which your race is well known. You have been your master's guardian and saviour. I am sure everyone will join me in congratulating you on your award, and we wish you many years in which to wear it.[1]

A year later Antis made his last trip by air, flying in a Dakota on a troop-carrying exercise over East Wretham. The airdrome was by then a ploughed field.

In August 1951, Jan was posted as an instructor to

[1] Extract from *The Animal Magazine:* the Official Journal of the People's Dispensary for Sick Animals: April 1949.

commissioned pilots at No. 8 Advanced Flying Training School at Dalcross, near Inverness. Man and dog were back in that country they knew and loved so well. The old Air Gunner's School at Evanton was close at hand.

1

It was a very fine day. Jan and his dog, on week-end leave from Dalcross, stood before the entrance to the camp site at Evanton. It had been something of an occasion, visiting old friends of the war years and staying at the local inn, where Antis had been remembered by crofters and villagers. And then his master's face became recognizable, though at first it had only stirred faint recollection.

Now they were back at the site of the old camp. All airmen were gone, but still Cnoc-Fyrish stood sentinel and the waters of Cromarty Firth danced in the sunlight.

An Air Ministry warden stood at the barrier. It took Jan's mind back to another warden and a Station Adjutant shaking with rage and a dark cellar in a cottage garden. But this was a pleasant and amiable man of formidable proportions, and when Jan explained his sentimental business, he readily allowed man and dog to pass, with the comment that he too liked to visit places he had known and loved. It made him, he said, feel happy and miserable at the same time, which was a very pleasant way of passing a nice October afternoon, in a manner of speaking.

So man and dog went into the camp and looked about them. The same avenue of trees, now autumnal tinted, led to the officers' mess, and the hutted lines still stood.

They passed down the lines and came to their old hut. The scratches of the dog's nails were still on the door. They entered and the hinges creaked, as of old. They found their room, but now it was grimed with neglect. It was difficult to imagine the four walls had ever contained

149

the semblance of a home. There was the musty smell of disuse.

They left the hut and made their way to the stream that flowed past the wood beyond the camp.

The mountain behind the tall trees rose stern and majestic. The amber water of the burn glistened and murmured. A solitary duck sailed by, with arrogant, wagging stern. The foliage and bracken were knee-high between the trees, but no small creature with bright eyes peered out at them. The old dog by Jan's side raised his muzzle whitened by age and sniffed the air. He began to whine very softly. He moved closer to his master because his sight was dim and there had been too many pangs of separation to endure another. Nothing must ever be lost again.

"We'll go home," said Jan sadly, and moved off slowly along the bank. The dog followed close at heel, his nose almost touching his master's leg. Once he faltered and looked back and whined again. The stream still murmured past Darreuch Wood, but even the duck was gone.

2

Always on Christmas Eve Jan set up the miniature Christmas tree. From where he lay in bed he thought it looked very pretty, with its tinsel and glittering artificial frost. He had also laid the photographs out beside the tree in recognition of the season. There was a photo of Tatiana in her wedding dress, another of Tatiana with little Robert in her arms, several of his mother and father, and one of the farm. Every Christmas the little tree and the photographs must be placed in precisely the correct position. It was the fifth Christmas now since he had been exiled from his native land for the second time. He wondered how many more there would be and if by this time next year he would be utterly alone. Thirteen years was a great age for a dog. He reached for the switch by his pillow and put out the light.

He supposed that he must have slept for some time because the stove had gone out. There was a weight on his chest, and when he stretched out his hand it came in contact with the loose folds of skin in his dog's neck. His fingers touched the collar, traveled onward, and found the ears. Antis was lying with his head on his master's breast.

This was unusual. Once the dog had retired for the night he could be trusted to lie on his blanket till the morning. Antis must have left his corner and crossed the room in the dark. Then he heard the dog sigh.

"What's the matter, boy?" said Jan. The sigh came again, tremulous, a little fainter.

"Go back to your bed," said Jan. He felt the weight of the dog's head lift slowly from his chest. Then there was the indeterminate scrabbling of his paws on the floor. The sound lacked the customary decisive patter. Jan thought to himself, he's getting very old. All at once there was the sound of a falling body.

Jan switched on the light. Antis lay on his side, full-length on the floor. His legs were twitching, as if he were attempting to rise, but the strength had gone from his limbs. He was panting with brief, shallow gasps, but his eyes were open. Jan flung aside the sheets and leaped out of bed and crossed to him. The dog must have cramp, he told himself. Cramp comes with old age. It was to be expected. He lifted Antis in his arms and carried him to his own bed and began to massage his legs.

It was only a temporary attack, Jan was certain. The old dog had overtaxed himself. He would have to be watched more carefully in future.

"It's all right, boy," said Jan. "It's going to be all right." He continued the massage. All through the night he continued the massage at intervals. At dawn he gave up the task. There was no change in the dog's condition. He carried him back to his corner.

By noon of Christmas Day the dog managed to stand

on his feet, but when Jan moved to the door and called to him to follow he was too weak to obey.

There were the usual day-long festivities, the sergeants' visit in the morning to the officers' mess, the attendance at midday by the officers at the airmen's mess, serving their Christmas dinner, and at night the spread in the sergeants' mess. Jan stayed with his dog.

By seven o'clock at night the hutments were deserted. From his window Jan could see the lights in his mess and hear the sound of laughter and singing. Twice friends looked in, brought a bottle and glasses, and asked how his patient was progressing, suggesting that he might be left for a while. Jan thanked them, took the drink, and bade them be on their way. Then he returned to his vigil. It was, he thought grimly, his turn now.

He sat by the table with the Christmas tree on it and took up Tatiana's photograph. She looked radiant in her wedding dress, and he remembered Antis had become entangled in her veil when they'd left the church and Gustav had come to the rescue. Now across at the mess they were playing "Silent Night." It was an old favorite of his. Dozens of Christmases they'd played it, at Tain and Evanton, at East Wretham and Honington. An old, old tune, and yet it was only yesterday that he'd heard it first. The room was full of ghosts, Karel and Joska, Ocelka and Pickard; there were scores of them trooping in. And soon there would be another one. It was of no avail to delude himself longer. One ghost more; the old dog was dying. Antis dragged himself from his bed and across the floor and lay outstretched with his head at his master's feet.

3

He lived till August. Radiant heat treatment, on a vet's advice, kept the dog alive, limping badly, with every step painful. His sight began to fail and he had difficulty in swallowing his food. Jan wrote to the People's Dispensary for Sick Animals asking what he should do. A telegram came back:

> DEEPLY SORRY TO HEAR NEWS. ADVISE PUTTING OLD FRIEND OUT OF MISERY. GRAVE RESERVED.

On August 11, 1953, Jan carried his dog to the operating theater at the Sanatorium at Ilford. With his head between his master's hands, sighing gently as the surgeon painlessly injected him, Antis, at the age of thirteen years and six months, closed his eyes for the last time.

He lies buried in the Animal Cemetery at Ilford.

Jan has never owned another dog.

If you enjoyed this book, you'll want to read these other exciting Bantam Pathfinder Editions